First off I want to thank everyone who actually spent their money on me in a struggling economy. As a first time Author I appreciate the opportunity to entertain you and expose my gift through my craft. I want my readers to understand I do not wish to glorify the criminal lifestyle in no shape way or form. I only wish to give you a visual through my words. I give you the real street literature I grew up on like Donald Goines. He started those gritty street tales that started another genre in literature. I came from those areas, went through the same struggles and still do to this day. I give you all sides of the game and every book as a positive a message. I just ask for all my young readers that are going through the struggles of growing up in these communities. Read urban fiction and watch the gangster movies for entertainment, not to mimic or portray. Chase your dreams and you can be anything in your life you want to be. My President is black, look at how a nation came together and changed a way of life. For two terms so it wasn't a fluke. People have paved the way for us and sacrificed so much for us to have the opportunities we have. Grind hard and believe in you, because that's where it starts first. Philly support Philly let's get it!!

Dedication

I want to dedicate this book, the first of 9 I wrote while incarcerated for 5 years, to my better half, Janae Allen. You held it down when they all left or didn't believe. You were still there holding on strong even though it was hard to do. You never gave up on me or my vision. I love you and my first book is dedicated to you. My other half, and my crutch, and the mother of my youngest child. You're a blessing...Let's make them even madder!

Chapter 1

The Start

Anthony was just like any other kid growing up in the inner city. He was poor and on welfare. His misfortune is what fueled his hunger to want more and strive for a better way of living. The only problem was his role models. They weren't his father, an Uncle or Grandfather to help and teach him along the way. He looked up to the hustlers in the hood, rappers in the videos, and all the flashy things that came with that luxury lifestyle.

At a young age he knew that he couldn't live like his mother, struggling to pay the bills, and to put food on the table. The dream Anthony wanted to see come true the most, was buying his mom a house and getting her out the ghetto. He just wanted her happy.

Anthony was what you would call a go getter. Since the years of middle school he was a hustler it came natural. He used to steal M&M's and Now& Laters from the corner store in West Philly. He used to take the M&M's and put 7 in a baggie and sell them for 10 cents apiece. He sold the Now& Laters for 10 cent also just 3 in a baggie. He always had a way with the girls since he was in diapers. His older sister Angie and his mother Betty Ann use to school him. "Don't let no big butt and a smile get you for ya money boy." His mom use to always say to him. His sister use to teach him the basics, her and her girlfriends. So he was a pro at kissing and rubbing the right spots since he was 10. They use to tell him. "Remember Ant don't be hype to get pussy that's a turn off. Not too hard and not too fast when kissing and touching her body." Then let him rub their breast and kiss their necks. Angie stayed around some young freaks and Anthony loved it and learned a lot.

"Ayo Ant whassup?" Ant's best friend Rome said as he walked up to the school. Ant was sitting outside of Shoemaker middle school waiting on his customers to cop up on his candy. "Ayo Ant you be out here like you on the block hustling waiting on some smokers!" Rome stated and laughed.

"Just because I'm selling candy don't mean I ain't no hustler. I'm about a dollar them girls don't like broke dudes. You gotta be able to pull that bread out and show that money!" Anthony pulled out a wad of cash that looked like a lot of money. The bankroll was 100 dollars in ones with a ten on top. Rome eyes grew wide at his young friend's money. "Well is you going to put me down or what nigga. I like money too!"

"Nigga you just gonna eat up all the candy! I know you bull! But if you need some cash I got you! You my best friend I can't have you broke." Anthony dug in his pocket and passed Rome off 25 dollars. "Show me you a hustler tho and turn that into 50!"

Maria walked up and waved at the boys. "Hey y'all!" Maria was in Anthony's math class and he had the biggest crush on her. He just didn't sweat her like the rest of his peers. "Damn she bad!" Rome said licking his lips. Maria was half black and Puerto Rican. Her hair was curly down her back and her small waist brought out her growing curves. "Maria when you going to give me ya number? I'm done playing with you babe?" Maria stopped in her tracks as she heard Anthony's remarks. "Whenever you ask all you do is look. Lookin don't get you no where wit me." She spat back at him.

"Well I'm asking now pretty thang."

"I will give it to you after math class. Oh and don't call me pretty thang. My name Maria make sure you know how to come at me or don't...until you ready." Anthony was shocked at the way Maria was talking to him. He never seen this bold sassy side and it turned him on.

"My bad baby I thought I could talk to my girl any way I wanted!" Maria smiled and put out her hand. "You crazy boy gimmie two packs of them M&Ms." Anthony passed her four packs and leaned in close to her ear. "That's on me baby!"

"I know it's on you silly, you my boyfriend right?" Maria wasn't a pretty push over, she had moved from Richard Allen Projects to 60th and Lansdowne. So she came up fighting girls there so to move to west she had two fights and earned her respect with the black girls. A few hated behind her back but none brought it her face because they had seen her in action.

"Damn bull that was smooth you better hit that!" Rome said watching Maria hip sway back and forth as she left.

"Sit back and learn something canon." Anthony made about 15 dollars before they both decided to get to class. Rome was always by Ant's side and as the years progressed they became tight as brothers. They were always down for each other. If you had a problem with one you had a problem with both.

After school let out at 3:15p.m it was always ruotine to chill outside of the school or go to the park. Today it was Ant, Rome, Maria and her friend Dallas. They met up after school and decided to go kick it at the park across the street from the Shoemaker. The park was right next to the playground and kids had already begun to play football in the field. Maria and Ant held hands as they walked around the playground area. Rome was talking to Dallas for a while until someone challenged him to play ball. He went right to the basketball court leaving Dallas to find Ant and Maria. Three shots rang out on the playground area and tires screeched. Ant grabbed Maria and covered her up on the ground as screams and footsteps running, was all he could hear. "Ant I'm scared," Maria whispered in his ear as he lay on top of her. "I got you babe just stay down!" Ant looked up and saw Kenny by the swings on the ground bloody. He was kicking his feet with the last amount of life he had left.

"Ayo Ant, we out bull c'mon!" Rome screamed from the basketball court. Ant and Maria got up and saw Dallas and Rome were together. They all ran from the scene and was grateful they didn't catch a stray. It was rough growing up in Philly, and Ant hated how many people he saw die already at his age. A dead body was normal and shoot outs seem like they happened every day.

"Ayo let's get these girls home bull!" Ant told Rome.

"That's fucked up they got Kenny. He just start hustling for big G. He was the only one in the class with the gold Jesus piece. Niggas was hating because he in the 8th grade getting money." Ant just shook his head and they walked the girl's home.

After the boys walked the ladies to Maria crib they made their way home.

"Yo bull I be thinkin sometimes I don't wanna die young." Rome stated sadly with his head down as they walked. Ant never really gave it a lot of thought it was a blessing where he came from to make it to see 18.

"Why you talkin like that nigga, you good?"

"Yeah for now nigga, this shit crazy out here. Kenny like the 5th person this year to get killed from our school. That's just our school. Ayo I don't wanna die young. I need a gun so I can protect us bull. I'm so serious I will pop the shit outta a nigga for tryna play us!" Rome put up his hands like he was shooting a gun. Anthony felt where he was coming from. It was kill or be killed this was the concrete jungle. Philadelphia, the city of brotherly love, but it wasn't nothing but hate there!

"Yo bull you my man and I'm ridin so if a nigga try you he try me. If we die young, a lot of niggas coming with us my nigga!" They shook hands and embraced as if they made a silent pact that day to never break.

When they got to the neighborhood they parted ways at the top of the block. Rome went to Hirst Street and Ant went down Felton. It was a large crowd of white t shirts in the middle of the block. Ant knew all the hustlers in the neighborhood from Wurt, Mildew, Skee, Brizz, Juice, Shake, and C.j. It was a dice game going on and it was some big money on the ground.

"Ayo Ant!" The familiar voice yelled from the crowd.

"Whassup C.J?" Anthony saw C.j emerge from the crowd with a hand full of money. "Damn lil nigga when you gonna let ya sister know I wanna holla? Take this and do that solid for me." C.j handed Ant a hundred dollar bill. Money from C.j wasn't nothing knew he always gave him 10 or 20 and told him stay in school and tell his sister he loved her. C.j had the hots for Angie but she wasn't with dealing with neighborhood boys.

"Good looking C.J I'm a tell her. You know she be drawin!"

"You a cool ass lil nigga! I always knew you was official. These other lil niggas wanna ride bikes and you on getting paper. I Like dat!"

"My mom and my sister say these girls don't want no broke nigga." They both started laughing and C.j shook his hand and Ant went to the house.

"Moooommms!" Anthony screamed when he walked in and slammed the door behind him. "What boy, don't be yelling in my house like that!"She said from the kitchen as she prepared dinner. Hotdogs and beans was on the menu for tonight. "Mom I found this on the corner I think it rolled from the dice game outside. Put it up with the rest of my money." Anthony passed her the hundred dollar bill with a smile.

"You know boy you be finding a lot of money. I'm going to start calling you lil Cash. Shit I might pay the rent with ya lil stash shit and save me some money for once."

"Mom I'm saving you can't spend it. I like that name you should call me that. Yeah lil Cash that's hot."

"Boy go clean ya room do that homework and wash up for dinner!"

"Mom can I go back out I will do that later?"

"Cash you better get ya ass upstairs and do what I told you!"

"Ard mom dang…" Anthony smiled hearing her call him Cash and did what he was told. He knocked his homework out and then he tossed everything in his closet and under the bed and his room was clean. The new lil Cash flew outside to greet the streets.

He headed toward the corner where the crowd was. He felt pround and some what a new person.

"Whassup lil nigga ya mom let you back out. What ya sister say?" C.j joked as he puffed the blunt hanging from his lip.

"My name lil Cash bull, don't call me lil nigga!"

"Oh shit my bad bull! Yo everybody listen up this my lil nigga Lil Cash he bout his paper! Now what ya sister say nigga?"

"She wasn't home." For the next few hours Cash and C.j talked about life, girls, and the streets. Lil Cash looked up to C.j because he was his own boss. He didn't work for anybody and he was young and getting it. At 22 C.j was already on half of a brick. He was on the block the most and when you was the guy out there all day everyday, you were bleeding the block. That's what the old heads use to say.

"Ayo C.j I wanna get that big money! How can I get out the hood I aint no ball player?" C.j looked at his young face and saw his sincerity.

"What you know about big money bull? You nothing but a six grader."

"I know I make 80 dollars in two weeks off candy I steal. Nigga that's 100% profit! So I know I can get these fiends to buy crack rocks!"

"Listen Lil Cash this shit ain't no joke out here. You gotta risk ya life and be ready to die for respect. The one time you show weakness your food. You ain't ready for the block yet stick to candy." He stood up and lifted his shirt. "Look... niggas ain't playing out here. I got hit last summer twice and thought I was done. You ready for this life lil nigga?" C.j said coldly as he showed off his war wounds that almost killed him last year. He told Lil Cash this because no one sat him down to warn him. He always wanted to play ball but after he got shot he jumped head first in the game. He had already been to jail, got shot, and lost a lot of friends to the game. C.j had lived a hard life and he was a product of his environment like so many others in his community. “So whassup you still want to be on the block after this talk?” C.j asked his young protégé.

“Hell no I never wanted to be a block boy! I wanna be the boss…I wanna run shit! I got money saved up how much can I get with 800?”

“Damn lil Cash you got 800? I can hook you up go get ya money and meet me at my spot in a hour. You know where my spot at right?”

“Yeah I know where it’s at!”

“Ard well go get ya money and don’t tell nobody what you doing. I got a ounce for you that’s 28 grams you should kill em with that. Ayo if ya sister home don’t forget to let her know I love her sexy ass.” Lil Cash agreed and headed home to get his money from the stash.

After getting the money from his house he went to Rome’s place. He sat down with his friend and told him everything C.j had told him. He wanted Rome to be right there with him to get this money.

“I’m with you until the end bro lets get it.” Rome stated meaning every last word.

“Ard I be back let me see ya bike I gotta go get the work.”

“Go head it’s in the back yard.” Lil Cash rode the bike to C.j’s spot and brought it up on the porch. He knocked two times. C.j grabbed his 357 and put it behind his back as he went toward the door. “Who is it?” He peeked through the window and saw Lil Cash by himself. “It's me Lil Cash open the door!” The door flew open and C.j told his lil homie to come in.

“Listen to me Cash. You gotta worry about a lot of shit on that block. Shit ain't sweet. You got jammy boys lurking, the undercovers dressed as smokers and ya momma! You fuckin up already tryna grind on the same block you live on.”

“Ayo C.j we already talked about this bull. I really aint tryna hear all this extra shit oldhead. I got my money!” Lil Cash pulled his savings out of his pocket and waved it in C.j's face.

“Say no more then. It's time for basic slinging 101. You ready cashmoney?”

“I was born ready bull.” C.j showed Cash the ounce and a razor blade. He showed Lil Cash how to bag up his drugs and get the most out of his product. C.j told Cash as long as his money was straight he would give him the work for 800 a O. Lil Cash ended up with 2000 dollars in nicks, he would make 1200 profit when he was done.

“Yo Cash don't run ya mouth about this.Just get ya paper and do something with ya life. You can't be a drug dealer forever it's not a career.” C.j tried to teach his young friend as much as he could, but at the end of the day it would be Cash's decision to make with his future. They always said the game was sold not told!

The first week of Cash's hustling he didn't realize how fast the money came. All he had to do was stand there and the smokers came left and right. Felton street did numbers in the mid and late 90's and C.j had the best work out there. That's why lil Cash showed he was a loyal hustler. He was saving his money as usual and when he went to school he stayed fresh to death. His wardrobe had made a drastic increase and the young ladies saw who was getting money. Cash had passed his game with the candy to his class mate Gary or Gmoney that's what Cash called him. He was real light skin and skinny. His stayed to hisself and didn't bother anyone.His clothes were bummy and Cash just wanted to see him come up. So he passed the game to him and hoped he helped him out. Cash hated to see people struggle and if he could he would help anybody that needed it, that's just the kind of heart he had.

The block had slowed down a little but Cash only had a few rocks left and it was getting late. Jimbo walked up he was a neighborhood smoker who always had something for sell. "What you need Jimbo I got them husky ass nicks!?"

"Man I'm fucked up lil Cash you know I would holla at you young blood."

"Solid so whassup ain't no credit poppin off you know I can't stand it!"

"Naw I got this 380 if you need a gun. You know you got to watch ya back out here. It's only a matter of time before somebody try you young blood." Cash smirked and and looked at the small pistol in Jimbo's hand. "I got 6 nicks for you right now whassup take it or leave it?" Lil cash needed a gun and a 380 was just his size. Jimbo was right it was only a matter of time and Lil Cash wanted to be prepared. Jimbo shook his head in agreement. "Just because I fucks with you. I see you got that fire in ya eye like a guy I use to do business with name Aaron jones. You might run this bitch one day here." Jimbo said as he passed the gun to Lil Cash and received his crack that eased his pain. He even gave Cash two clips for it on the strength. "Oh I forgot I got a Burnout too if you tryna buy it." A burn out was a cellphone that didn't have a bill or add minutes. It lasted 3 to 6 months then you throw it away. "I got 3 nicks for it."

"Shit we got a deal here you go." Jimbo passed the phone off and received his illegal medicine. Cash didn't waste any time. He tucked his gun in his waist band and dialed Maria's number. "Hello can I speak to Maria please?" Cash always spoke politely when calling some one's home, especially a girl. It gained him cool points with the parents. "It's me who is this?"

"It's ya boyfriend how many other niggas you got callin?"

"Well I didn't know I still had a boyfriend. You don't come to school anymore and I haven't heard from you in weeks!" Cash couldn't lie all his time was being consumed by the block. School had been last on his list. He had saved $4900 in little over a month. School wasn't producing that. School wasn't getting his mom out the hood. With the time he spent hustling he thought about what he was stacking for. He told his self once his mom was good he would open up a night club. All the hustlers were always talking about going to the club to ball and pop bottles. He thought why not own that club they wanted to spend their money in. He was still young so as long as he stayed focus and saved his money he would be financially stable in the future. "Baby I'm sorry I been working my ass off. I promise I will pick you up on Friday."

"When you get a car?"

"I don't have one my old head gonna let me see his jawn. Last day of school Friday right?"

"Yeah pick me up at 12."

"Ard baby I see you Friday." Cash hung up and dialed Rome and told him to get to the block. It didn't take him long to come from around the corner smoking a joint. "Yo bull my peoples left this in the ashtray you want some?" Rome asked as he approached his friend. Cash pulled out the 380 and passed it off to Rome. He grabbed the gun and held it tightly. "Yo bull where you get this jawn from?"

"Jimbo looked out for me. I called you around here cuz I need you."

"Nigga whatever you need you know you my bro.Whassup?"

"You my right hand and you been a gun since I met you. I never seen you back down from nobody and you always had my back. So take dat hold it down and be my gun. Lay niggas down that get outta pocket. We aint looking for beef, but we aint duckin it either!"

Rome put the gun in the small of his back under his shirt. He gave cash a firm hand shake and pulled him in for a hug. "Let's get it my nigga! I swear on my momma if a nigga cross us he outta here. Let's eat!"

Friday came and C.j had did what he said and let Cash see one of his cars. He was blasting Beanie Sigel who was like what Biggie was to Brooklyn in Philly at the time. Cash was playing Die off the Truth Lp and he knew every word. When he pulled up in front of Shoemaker middle it was almost 12, so he rolled up some dro and sparked a blunt while he waited.

The school let out and all the kids rushed the exits to say hello to summer vacation. Maria and Dallas saw Cash smoking in the car in front of the school. "C'mon Dallas he will take you home!" They walked over to the car as Cash blew smoke from his nose. "Baby can you drop Dallas off for me?" cash looked at Dallas in those tight Guess jeans and licked his lips. "No problem babe you know Dallas my mistress." Cash joked and they piled up in the car. As they rode toward Dallas house his phone rang. "Hello, yeah, alright, she'll be there in a minute." He hung up the phone and looked over at Maria. "That was ya mom talking fast as hell with that Spanish shit. She said get dat ass home right now babe." Cash quickly made a U turn and headed to Maria's house he didn't want any problems with her mother. When they pulled up to her house Cash got out to get in the trunk. He got the bag from Footlocker and passed it to Maria. "I got you the new Jordan's babe and some nike jawns too." Maria gave him a wet kiss and hugged him tightly. "Thank you, thank you, thank you!" Maria said as she planted his face with kisses. He even put 200 in her pocket, she was in love and as long as he treated her like this she would be losing her virginity real soon.

She said goodbye to Dallas and went in the house. "Get ya ass up front yo!" Dallas got out and got in the passenger seat, and Cash drove off. "Don't talk to me like dat little Cash. I ain't no lil girl." Dallas popped her gum and continued. "That was nice of you to get those shoes for Maria. She lucky."

"I do whatever I can for my girl's."

"Girls?" She asked confused only thinking he had Maria.

"Yeah like my sister, mother, girlfriend, and every girl I deal with."

"This my house on the corner but drive around let's talk!"

Dallas was older then Cash and Maria by two years that was her last year at Shoemaker, and next year she would be a freshmen at Overbrook high school. Her mom smoked crack and her father was doing 20 years in prison. She basically raised herself and pushed herself to finish school. Her mother was never home so she had freedom to do what she wanted and stay out as late as she wanted, her mom didn't care. So at 14 she was already sexually active. When Dallas told him to just drive he felt she was up to something. Rome had already told him that Mike and Jason said they hit it and she was a freak. For the first time he started to really look at her as he drove. Her smooth brown skin and full lips were attractive. Her hair was shoulder length and she had a nice size bubble that hypnotized any eyes that watched it. "Pull over right here." Cash pulled over on the small block she pointed out and cut the car off. "Cash would I be wrong if I said I like you?" She placed her hand on his thigh and felt his penis jerk in his jeans. "You wouldn't be wrong you would be real if that's how you feel D."

"Pull it out Cash…let me see it." Her voice was filled with lust and it started to get hot. "You pull it out!" Cash said as he pulled his seat back to see what she would do. Dallas licked her lips and unzipped his pants. She pulled his dick out and slowly stroked it while locking eyes with him. She spit on it and started to jerk faster. "HMMMMMM…Cash let out a moan and Dallas took him in her mouth. Both her hands clutched his dick as she sucked him hard up and down and still jerking him at the same time. The feeling was unbelievable, it felt so good. He gripped the back of her head and made her suck faster as she bobbled up and down on his shaft. "Oh shit I think I'm bout to nut…ahhhh….oh shit suck that dick!!!" Dallas didn't skip a beat and as Cash erupted she swallowed. She came up for air with her hair looking wild from him gripping it so tight. "You ready for the pussy Cash or you done?" This was actually his second time getting head and he was still a virgin. He had been waiting for Maria but Dallas was ready now and his dick was still rock hard. He looked at his throbbing member and looked back at Dallas. She went right back down on it with those soft lips and before he knew it she was riding him right there in the car. This is what pussy feel like huh. This is the shit! I can't believe I'm fucking Dallas right now. I'm sorry Maria baby I'm sorry! His thoughts raced as the sound of Dallas pussy juices splashing in his lap. "Oh God Dat dick feel so good!" She bounced up and down as they fogged up the windows and went at it for another 30 minutes. Cash and Dallas both were exhausted and the car really didn't have any space. "Let's go to my house my mom don't care who I bring over. We can do it in my bed." Dallas kissed his neck grabbed his deflating penis and waited for a response. "We out but yo... Don't tell Maria this shit will kill her."

"I won't that's my girl...now c'mon cuz I want some more dick!" She pulled Cash in for a wet kiss.

Chapter 2

Moving Up In The Game

Cash and Rome had been hustling none stop for a year. Lil Cash and Rome left school and dedicated their time to getting money. Cash still stuck to his plans and saved the majority of his money. Rome on the other hand was buying whatever he wanted. He didn't have plans on the future he was living for today. He had already purchased two hoopties an old school Chevy Camaro and 1995 Acura. His closet was over filled with the hottest urban wear and he had over a hundred pair of sneakers. Cash had kept it low key he stayed with some fresh Timberland boots and a Dickie suit, or white t and jeans. He had to get a hoop so he got a 1997 Maxima.

Cash turned on Felton and saw Rome, Wurt, and Mildew on the block posted. He parked and stepped up on the curb with his homies.

"What's good wit ya'll niggas?" Everybody said hello and Rome pulled him to the side. "Let me holla at you real quick." Rome pulled the black and stainless steel .40 cal from under his Throwback Eagles jacket.

"Look what I grabbed bull!" Rome was excited and Cash always remembered that look in his eye when he gave him the 380. Every time he had a gun he kept that look and that's why he started collecting them. Rome was always strapped. "This jawn nice." Cash held it in his hand and clutched it.

"That's you I got two of em." Rome pulled another from his waistband.

Cash started laughing. "You got 50 guns on you damn. Good lookin tho I need dis jawn." Lil Cash tucked the gun and look around to see who was watching. As the day progressed it got late and Rome and Lil Cash was on the only two hustling. Rome was sitting on the stoop counting his money. "Damn I lost 400 in the dice game and still made 1500 out here. Yo this work some oils."

"I know lets be out tho its slow now. I'm tryna get some Haze, call da bull up." Rome looked up and down the block and noticed a fiend coming toward them.

"Let me get this last smoker and we out." The man got closer and was fumbling with something. Rome couldn't see until it was too late and the gun was in his face. "Don't move youngbulls!!! Run it…take that fuckin jacket off and empty ya pockets. Crack and money reach for anything else and my finger gonna slip cuz I'ma get nervous and ya friend head gonna have a sun roof." Rome just stood there with his nose just centimeters from the barrel and started taking his 500 dollar jacket off. Cash wanted to reach for his gun but he didn't want to risk it.

He started dropping money on the ground. Rome seen his right hand man giving up all that money, and he snapped out of his quiet stage.

"Hold the fuck up bull. Do you know us, we from around here this our block? Are you high right now nigga?!! We aint giving you shit pussy!" Rome went for his weapon. BOC BOC!!

The smoker let off two shots that ripped through Rome's legs."AHHHHHHHH SHHHITTTT!!!" The man stood over his body looking at Cash in his eyes as he was about to take his best friend off the planet. "Wait!!! Take the money bull it aint that deep and the jacket. You better pray I never see you again nigga. Philly small you remember that." Cash went over to Rome and put pressure on his wounds. The fiend smiled with an evil grin and Cash saw two brown front teeth and the gun now in his face. "Fuck you lil nigga!" He picked up the money and grabbed the jacket still pointing it in Cash's face. "I can't feel my legs Cash!!! I can't feel my fuckin legs!!!" Rome screamed and Cash looked in his bleeding friends eyes and didn't know what to do. He looked back at his robber but he had run down the block. Cash had both his hands on the wounds of Rome that were leaking extremely bad. He called 911 and all they could do was wait. In this area the cops and ambulance were close but always took forever. "Yo bull roll up!" Cash looked at Rome who had tears in his eyes and they had to laugh. The ambulance took 34 minutes to get to them and Rome was high as a kite and couldn't feel nothing. When they put him in the back of the ambulance he sarcastically said. "You guys have speedy service real shit you deserve a raise." The hospital ride Cash just thought of that face and those two brown teeth who had his life in his hands. He hated that feeling and if he ever saw that man again it was on sight. Rome was fine the bullets went right through. He would be on crutches and would fully heal in a few months. The doctors asked him lots of questions.They started with who he lived with, and where were his parents. Rome was a loner after his dad got life and his mom overdosed he was dumped on his crack head Uncle John. The doctors were curious what a young boy would be doing out so late to get shot. His Uncle came up the next day and wheel chaired his nephew right outta there and back home.

As Rome healed Cash held it down extra hard on the block and wasn't taking any chances he kept his gun on him. The encounter with death just fueled Rome's fire to go hard in the streets. When he could fully walk right he would be back, until then Cash was dolo out there. He was pulling all nighters to get bacjk the money he and Rome got stuck up for. His phone vibrated and the caller i.d read Maria. "Hello, oh really, don't tell me that I be there in a minute!"

Maria parents were out of town to Atlantic City for the night and she wanted company. He knew it was about that time all the kissing and rubbing was getting old. Dallas and him was still sexing on the regular behind her back so his skills were tight. Since Dallas, he had sex with a few other girls but Dallas was everyday. They couldn't get enough of each other the bond was incredible. Cash parked the hoop infront of her house and went to knock on the door but it swung open. Maria had her hair down and nothing on but that gold ankle bracelet. Cash bit his bottom lip, the view instantly made his dick throb. "Baby c'mere." Cash walked over to her and she started to take off his clothes. Maria noticed the gun on his hip. "Baby let me see?" She pulled it out and held it with both hands.

"Chill babe you too bad to be poppin niggas let me do that for you." He took the gun and placed it on the coffee table. Cash wasn't having it. He lifted her up and she sat on his shoulders while he tasted her sweetness. Her moans were loud and fierce she clawed the top of his head as he stuck his long wet tongue in her deeper. She couldn't believe how wet she was as she squirted out her very first orgasm. "HMMMMMMMM....AHHHH!! Oh my fuckin God Cash do it again baby!"

"I got you." He came out of his jeans and boots fast and stood infront of her face in his boxers. "Caaaassssshhhh stop teasin me papi! Maria pulled his boxers down with force and nose dived toward his penis. SLURP SSSLLLL SLURP SLLLLURP!!! The loud sounds of her spit as she sucked him hard taking him deep in her throat. "Oh shit! Damn what the fuck?" Cash humped away at her face as she cuffed his buttocks to force more in her. He didn't want to cum yet. He pulled out of her mouth and turned her around on the couch. She arched her back and looked back at him with it in the air. Cash stepped up and in the pussy he went. It was tight and juicy he stroked slow and from the slight blood on his dick he noticed the cherry was popped. "That shit feel so goooood!" He gripped her hips and her muffled screams in the couch pillow were still loud. Maria was in paradise and she threw it back at him as he stroked.

"CASH FUCK ME! I'm used to it now FUCK ME!" Maria put her face deep in the couch and Cash hammered away. Maria was humming and moaning at the same time while Cash gave her long heavy back shots. "Arrrrggggghhhhh........awww shit!" Cash came and flopped over on the couch exhausted. "Shit!" Maria laid her head on his sweaty chest as both their hearts were beating rapidly. "Baby that dick gooood!" They passed out and Cash awoke at 3a.m to 8 missed calls all from Dallas. He shook Maria and kissed her lips as she awoke. "I gotta go baby I'ma see you tomorrow Rome need me." Maria was dead tired she said I love you and went right back to sleep. Cash hopped in his car and headed to Dallas house. She never called him this much he knew something was up. It wasn't any traffic this late so he got there in ten minutes. As he used his key to come in she was on the couch in the dark. "Whassup why you blowing me up? And why you in here in the dark?"

He noticed she was crying from the dried up tears all down her cheeks.

"I'm pregnant Cash…I'm pregnant!" She burst out in tears and began to weep and cry. Cash knew he never wore a condom but that didn't stop him from asking. "So who the daddy?"

"Fuck you pussy it's yours!! You know since we been fuckin I only had sex with you. Fuck you Cash!" He stood there and just shook his head he wasn't ready for a kid he was just a kid his self. Cash punched the wall and left a nice crack in it and stormed out the house without saying anything to Dallas.

Cash hadn't seen Rome in a while, it hurt his heart to not see his homie walking yet. He still passed his cut off of the flip and tucked his stash money for him. They were partners and Cash would never not give Rome is cut. This was really a time he needed to just sit down with him and talk. C.j had been dating Angie now so all his time was with his sister. C.j hadn't been hustling on the block in months he stayed up under Angie all day every day. He was what the streets called a sucka for love ass nigga! So when Wurt and Mildew and the rest of the older dealers weren't out posted Cash was there.

When he was just floating in his car he got calls on his cell and made drop offs. The money was flowing but the problems were coming right along with it. Cash had a sell on Maria's block so he flew through there slowly puffing as usual some killa that was 500 a ounce. He noticed some guys all crowded on Maria's step. They all were laughing and joking. Cash wasn't feeling the vibe he didn't like his girl all up in guys faces. That was a no no. He parked up and took his piece from under the seat and tucked it in his waist. He wasn't about to shoot them he just wanted to make sure they didn't make him shoot them. "Hey baby I didn't know you was coming pass." Maria went to kiss him as he approached and he put his hand up to block her. "What the fuck is this a girl scout meeting? Everybody all laughing and shit gathering around. Y'all know this my girl right?" By this time Lil cash was growing a name for his self as a get money young gun. The two young dudes didn't want any trouble they really didn't mean any harm they were just conversing. "Yeah we know bull aint no beef we was just kickin it." The taller of the two added.

"I know it aint no beef cuz if it was you would be in a bag right now pussy! Get the fuck outta here before I slap da shit out you. My bitch off limits to talk to you can't converse unless it's beneficial." Since the robbery Cash had been waiting for somebody to get outta order so he could blow they top off. He needed to release some anger and he thought bussing his gun would give him his relief he craved for. In his mind he knew that these little guys didn't have anything to do with it and he was just angry and on edge. "We cool, we cool." The two kids backed up in defeat they both were 17 the same age as Cash. "You got me out here ready steal one of these niggas over you. Why you being all joe?"

"Shut up baby you know I only love you they my friends from around the way." She kissed his lips and they talked on her steps for a few minutes. "Ayo Cash!!" A voice from down the street yelled. He looked up and didn't recognize the face. "Who the fuck is ths another one of ya boyfriends?" He asked Maria as he went under his shirt and the guy got closer.

"Baby that's them boys brother he be drawin he always wanna fight or shoot some shit up. He swear he tough!"

"Yo bull you talkin reckless to my lil brothers? We got a problem cuz they not in the streets but I am?" This was Tone he was from 59th and Master.

Tone was a local hot head that wasn't known for getting money, just for being in the way.

"I just told them to stay away from my girl. Why whassup you wanna box or shoot it out. You coming off like you wanna do something?" Cash stood up with his hand under his shirt Tone was coming off too aggressive.

"Naw I just--- Tone hit Cash with a swift jab to his chin catching him off guard. Tone had him by 20 pounds and he was 22. Cash tasted blood from his split lip and was enraged. "You bitch ass nigga you snuck me?" Cash spit out blood. He countered and came from the waist with his gun smacking him in the face with it knocking him to his knees. "You like that!!" Cash put the gun back in his waist and spit blood once again.

"I'ma beat ya ass I aint even gonna shoot you." Cash hit him with a fury of blows as he tried to get up off his knees but was knocked back down.

"Get up nigga!" Cash allowed him to get his self up and put his guard up.

"Yeah that's right where ya hands at?" Tone went for a lazy hook and missed. Then a weak two piece that Cash dipped and came back with a hard right knocking him on his back pockets. He gets back up as he noticed a crowd form and they had spectators. Tone had a headache and was dizzy. He staggered getting in his stance. He felt his forehead and the gulf ball knot he had was throbbing. Cash came in close and went to work on the body, left right, left right. Then he went up top and hit the gulf ball with a heavy left hook knocking him back out. Cash didn't wait for him to get up he just went for the stomping. Kicks to the face and ribs until Tone was unconscious. Blood was over his boots he had snapped and Tone looked bad. He told Maria to get in the house and he got in the car and sped off. The life he chose was getting intense it seem the drama was always coming.

Too much was going on, he had to see Rome. So he found his self walking through his door. “Shit real nigga I Don’t know what to do?” Cash came in and sat down on the couch. Rome had his feet propped up in the lazy boy. His healing was coming along well. His friend looked disturbed and then he saw his footwear all bloody. “Yo bull whassup with ya boots? Who you check without me I know you aint find that crackhead Cash?”

“Naw nigga I just stomped some niga out that snuck me. Fuck these boots I got Dallas pregnant nigga!”

“Damn my nigga you don’t believe in rubbers? That’s ya fault you can’t get stressed now. We from where fathers don’t make it so you know what I’ma say.We raising ours! We not killing our seeds.” They talked about life, having kids and the future as grown men. Cash phone rang and it was back to the block. Cash gave his friend a hand shake and went to the block to chase that paper. When Cash parked on Felton he saw C.j out therewhich surprised him, it had been a while since he saw him posted.

“Okay bull I see you outta my sister ass whassup with you.” Cash said as he gave his old head a handshake. “I can afford to fallback lil Cash remember that. A real boss make sure we all eat.” Cash shook his head in agreement. “I gotta go scoop my big cousin Bonez take this ride I got some haze, Cash said waving the blunt in his hand. "We out!" C.j hadn't smoked any weed all day he was geeking.

Bonez lived down 40th and Parkside. He wasn't a street dude at all but he stayed in his lane. He got at the ladies and was an aspiring rapper. Some called him a pretty boy because he was light skin with good hair. Growing up he had to fight so his hands became nice. Cash just loved to chill with his family because these days you here today and gone tomorrow. "Whassup with y'all?" Bonez said as he got in the back seat of the cloudy car filled with haze smoke.

"We chillin where the hoes at cuz?" Just as Bonez was about to respond he saw the look on his Cousin's face. "Get the fuck outta here!!"

"Whassup cuz whats wrong?"

"There go the crackhead right there and he still got my nigga jacket on!!" He pointed to the Guy smoking a cig in front of Spiro's Pizza.

"Ayo Cash how you wanna do this bull? It's broad day light right now.My nigga, its people outside think!" C.j was always ready to ride for his people but he wasn't stupid. He wasn't trying to take a ride to get 30yrs.

"Nigga this the nigga right here fuck dat we airin him right here nigga!He shot my man he not getting away!" Cash barked.

"Fuck dat!! I'm a pull up, pop the trunk and we toss his bitch ass in. I know we can't off him right here on some dumb shit."C.j added trying to get Cash to understand the severity of what they were doing. It wasn't anymore thinking or questions, Cash was pulling up infront of the pizza shop. He popped the trunk and the all got out at the same time. “Bonez you drive, go head!” The man was smoking that cigarette to the green line he never paid attention to C.J at the payphone and cash coming right up on him.

“Can I get a light old head?” Cash walked up close and put his gun to his ribs and whispered in his ear. “I told you Philly too small nigga, now walk with me before I blow ya whole stomah out ya back! Think I'm playing!”

The crackhead's eye's almost came out of his head when he saw the young boy he robbed awhile back when he was high off PCP, or what they called it in Philly, wet. He had dipped 3 Newports that night and was tripping and needed money. He didn't think he would see this youngen again. “Yooooo don't do this youngbull don't do this!” He said as Cash calmly guided him toward the open trunk. C.j looked around and Cash really didn't cause a scene. “Get in!” They stood eye to eye infront of the trunk. The smoker felt the gun in his stomach and looked back in the trunk. “Please man, don't do this!” C.j walked over and hit him with a hard hook to the jaw knocking him right out and he was sleep before he hit the trunk floor. Cash closed the trunk and they both hopped in as Bonez pulled off. “This nigga Rome gonna snap when he see this nigga. Ayo Bonez drive this motherfucka!” Cash yelled from the back seat with his gun in his hand ready to put a bullet in this coward in the trunk.

KNOCK KNOCK KNOCK!!! The hard knocks to Rome's front door awoke him from his nap on the the couch. “Who the fuck? Its open nigga!” C.j walked in with a crazy look on his face.

“Who all in here?”

"Nobody is here nigga. Why you lookin all paranoid in the face?" C.j went to the door and said bring him in. When Cash and Bonez came in they had the crackhead that shot him. Rome got up on his crutches and hopped over to him. Cash had his gun in his back and he watched as Rome hopped over with a vicious glare. "Look what the fuck we got here boys." Rome gave him a stiff jab busting his nose. "Take him to the basement."

"Ayo C.j me and Rome gonna handle this. Take Bonez to the crib and hit my phone when you outside." C.j shook his hand firmly. "I got you bull."

Cash had tied the crackhead up in the basement and he and Rome stood over him with their guns drawn. This moment would change their lives.

"Don't do it yo I was high!! I'm fuckin sorry I swear to God don't kill me! I got 4 kids." Cash ran over to him as his hands and feet were tied behind his back. "Pussy!!" He let his boot meet his teeth and knocked out three from the mighty blow.

"ARRRRGGHHHH!!" The crackhead yelled in agony as blood spilled from his mouth. Cash stepped back and aimed.

"You ready for this bro?" Rome clutched his gun and hopped closer. He put the gun to his head and pulled the trigger. This was their first body, they stood there and watched as the smoke came from their victims scull and he laid lifeless. They both realized it wasn't any turning back now. They had took a person's life. They were gangsters…and at this moment Rome only knew one way. GO HARD!

Chapter 3

Two Is Better Than One

It had been three months and Cash had been ducking Dallas calls. He had too much on his mind and that situation wasn't in his equation. His time had been consumed with hustling and keeping him and Maria's relationship tight. Ever since they had sex Cash couldn't get enough of her. Rome was back on the block with his partner in crime. His legs fully healed and he was focused on the task at hand…Get money! Rome started to save his cash and he finally slowed down with being flashy. He didn't want another encounter of a gun in his face and someone taking something from him. A valuable lesson he learned early in the game.

Cash was keeping his circle tight and in this game you had to. He was only dealing with C.j, Rome and his cousin Bonez. Cash saw that with the money that was coming in friends become envious and family become jealous. A certain amount of money would have your mother stealing from you. So to avoid the drama he moved out and got his own apartment close to the hood.

"Baby can you take me to the mall?" Ever since Maria seen that Cash was really getting money she always hit his pockets. If it was a trip to the mall twice a week, or a few hundred for her pocket .Cash never told her no because he was doing so much wrong.

"I'm around the corner now you ready?"

"Yeah baby!" He pulled the blunt from the ashtray and fired it up as he pulled up in front of her house. He beeped his horn and she appeared from her house with Dallas right beside her. Cash jaw hit the floor he hadn't seen her in months she had just called yesterday and he ignored the call as usual. She was 4 months pregnant and showing that baby bump.

"Open the door Cash!" Maria barked helping Dallas down the steps.

"I'm cool girl, he aint gotta open the door for me!" He was just stuck starring at her belly until Maria snapped him back to reality. He quickly got out and opened the back door for Dallas so she could get in. Cash was acting funny when he started to drive he hadn't turned up the music or said a word. He kept both hands on the wheel and his eyes forward. "What's wrong with you? Baby is everything alright? You're acting weird."

"Nothing my head just hurt that weed taste funny." Cash tossed the blunt out the window and looked at Dallas in his rearview.

"Damn D ya stomach getting big girl?"

Dallas sucked her teeth and rolled her eyes. "Duh that's what happens when you get pregnant little Cash. I wish my baby father step up but he don't want shit to do with us."Dallas said sadly and Maria jumped right in.

"That's a bitch ass nigga right Cash? Only suckers don't take care of their kids!"

"I don't know they business and I don't want to Maria! You never know he might come around shorty!" It got quiet for a minute before cash spoke again. "When we done in the mall I'm getting a tat.Let me know if you coming or you want me to drop y'all off."

"We cool we can go!" Dallas said and Cash turned up the music as they drove toward King of Prussia mall.

When the trio got to the mall Maria was ready to shop she was quick to get out. Cash sat in the driver seat and saw Maria hand reach in.

“Baby gimmie some money.” He shook his head with a smile and dug in his pocket. Dallas watched from the back seat as Cash pulled a wad of bills from both pockets and sat it on his lap.

“Hold up chill for a sec.” He lifted his arm rest and pulled another bankroll about 5 inches thick of all twenty dollar bills. He started to count and Dallas was counting every bill with him trying to keep up. He finally finished and Dallas had counted $7400 dollars over his shoulder. “How much you need?”

“I don’t know just give me some babe?” Cash gave her 40 dollars. Maria grabbed it and threw it back on the seat and playfully hit him.

“Stop fuckin playin wit me Cash I aint one of them hood rats. Gimmie!” She snatched more than half the money on his lap and slapped his penis through his jeans. “Ouch!! Ayo chill you play too much.”

“You do too! C’mon Dallas lets go girl.” She waved the money in her face as she stood outside the car smiling at Dallas.

“Girrrrllll my stomach hurtin now my baby didn’t like that pizza roll. Go head I’m a wait in the car Maria.”

“You sure? Cash stay with her and don’t light up no weed she pregnant! I be back!!” Maria turned around and switched her happy self, inside the mall. Dallas watched as Maria got all the way in and smacked Cash in the back of the head hard.

"So you're fucking ducking me now. I'm just some bitch you fucking? This aint ya baby nigga? Turn around and look at me. You don't fuck with me and ya baby?" Dallas said with teary eyes and bass in her voice. Cash turned around and wanted to hug her so he pleaded his case.

"I'm sorry shorty…real shit I didn't want this to be like this. I'm fucked up cuz I'm stuck, like y'all friends what you want me to do I'm fuckin sorry! Fix it and I'm with it!!! We can't fix it! This situation fucked up. The shit hurt cuz I really really fuck with you but that's my girl… in there!!!" He pointed to the mall and they just looked at each other speechless.

Dallas shook her head and grabbed his hand and placed it on her stomach. She wanted him to feel the life that they created together.

"Look Cash I love you, and I know, that's my bitch. I love Maria!! This shit is fucked up. But I'm carrying ya baby and I love you… we can make us work and be a family." Cash felt his unborn son move and he knew he couldn't get him aborted. This was his son, his flesh and blood. He just couldn't figure out how to tell Maria and still have her in his life because that was where his heart was.

"You feeling that lil baby!! Don't it feel weird baby?" Maria walked up with bags and was at the passenger window. Cash was lost in the moment he didn't know he was just holding her stomach mesmerized.

"Yeah that's crazy I didn't know they felt like dat. Let me get them bags for you." Cash popped the trunk, Dallas pulled her shirt back down, and Maria passed her bags off.

"Lets go get tatted!" Maria said and got in the passenger seat. The ride back was quiet Maria was on her cellphone checking her Myspace and Dallas was struggling to keep it together in the back seat with a smile. Cash was battling with his heart and his gut. They pulled up at the tattoo parlor on 63rd and Market and Maria was hype, she knew she was getting one. Cash already had his mind made up so he didn't have to look at any pictures. He saw the guy in the back who was free and flagged him over.

"Yo canon I know what I want how much?" He said with his money in his hand. The shop was fairly crowded but like everywhere in this world. Money talks and bullshit walks! The older white guy with the beer belly who had the demeanor of a biker stepped from the back.

"What you lookin to get bro!?"

"I want Cash on my left hand with a big money bag. Then on my right hand a ski mask with Rome." Maria made a face like she bit a lemon and quickly interjected. "Eww why you getting Rome name on you that's gay?"

"That's my right hand so that's where he going." Cash answered.

"And whatever these ladies want but I'm going first."

"I want Cash on my neck!" Maria blurted out. She didn't care what nobody said about her baby, she loved her some Cash!

After about two hours Cash and Maria were done. The ink work was great and Cash went to drop Dallas off and take Maria to Rome house for a quickie. Rome was on the couch playing X-box while his homie was upstairs laying it down. He could hear Maria's moans and groans from all the way in the living room.

The sex Maria and Cash shared was passionate. He really loved her so he always put his all into it. His aim was to please her and it felt great doing it. Maria had to be home soon because her mom did not play with being out all night on a school day. The duo came from upstairs with the satisfied faces. Maria hair was a little out of place and her shirt was wrinkled. “All y'all do is fuck! Do y'all ever just watch a movie?” Rome joked still into his game on PS2. “Look nigga you my right hand!” Cash showed off his new ink. “That shit hot bro! Yo bull I'm on it, they gonna haaaatttee!” Rome said admiring his friend's tattoo. “You joe as shit Rome but look at mine!” Maria pulled her collar down and Rome shook his head. “Dats hot!”

“I'm out bull I got to drop her off and go see mom dukes, I be back.” Cash told Rome and he and Maria was out the door. It had been awhile since he sat down with his mom so he went straight there after he dropped Maria off. He tasted those lips before saying goodnight. Then he watched her go inside before he pulled off. “That's my fuckin baby!” Cash thought to himself.

“Mom!” Cash yelled as he came through the door. His mom was doing great.He was hitting her off with stacks of money every week like he was paying a tab off. He didn't want for her to need a man for anyhing. She went back to school with Cash's heavy deposits every week. She was getting her realtor license. She told Cash Real Estate would make the family rich, if she had the money and the legit schooling. So he was behind her 100%.

“Boy don't be yelling in my damn house!” She said watching Law and Order with her feet up and a glass of wine. Cash gave her a hug and kiss and sat down on the couch. “Look at my tat.” She shook her head.

"That was real dumb why you get another boy name on ya hand Anthony Miller?"

"Maria got my name on her neck."

"Well you should of got hers. Y'all kids these days I swear."

"Where Angie big head at?"

"She somewhere with C.j you know he be beating her ass. He be beating her like a nigga beating her ass! He fuckin crazy! I told her tell you, but she said don't but her eye right now is horrible." Cash couldn't believe what he just heard. His homie, his oldhead, his friend was beating his sister like she was a man. This wasn't happening, he got light headed. This wasn't the truth, it couldn't be. His thoughts raced and he finally spoke.

"Where they at now?"

Betty sipped the rest of her wine and looked in her young son's face which was starting to look old. She knew he sold drugs and she wasn't proud of it. But she never had nothing and always made a way so her kids could have. He provided and took care of the family and even if she ever did say Cash stop hustling. She knew he was too deep in and stuck in his ways. He had become a street guy right in front of her eyes.

"I don't know baby but whatever you do…don't be stupid you hear me? Don't be stupid just be careful and think because I know you love your sister. But you have a family that need you here. "Fuck it always something." He stood up infuriated. "Niggas always gotta force my hand." He let out a sigh and left out the house. His next stop was Rome's house. He broke down what his mom told him and he couldn't believe it. "I got this tho bull. Watch this." Cash called C.j on his cellphone. C.j had just dropped Angie off at his condo and was at his stash spot getting some things situated before he called it a night. "Yo bull where you at I need to holla at you bro?" C.j told him where he was not thinking there was a problem. Cash and Rome flew right over. The ride was quiet all he had on his mind was why his sister? When they walked in C.j's stash house he was bagging up some work at the table. Cash calmly walked over as if nothing was bothering him. BAM BAM BAM!!!! Cash start swinging and was connected with every blow to C.j's face. "You like beatin up females huh. My fuckin sister? Is you crazy nigga?" Cash hit him with another vicious 3 piece. C.j was caught off guard and every blow was picking him up and putting him right back down again. Cash pulled the gun from his hip and came across C.j's jaw with it hard. You could hear his bone crack as his face flew sideways. Cash follows up with a knee to his stomach taking his wind from his body. He couldn't even scream.

"Why yo, what she do?" Cash kicked him in the back as he layed on the floor hurt. Cash just needed to know the truth. C.j was his oldhead and this was serious.

"Ahhhhhhh shit!!! She cheated Cash!!! She cheated on me and I snapped one day, I just snapped, she was too disrespectful! My nigga…in my crib…in my bed!!" Tears streamed down his cheeks. He was heartbroken.

"I whooped her ass! I'm sorry! I couldn't stop myself my nigga. I love her so much!" C.j cried out as Cash aimed the gun at him standing over his body. Cash looked him in the eye and fired the gun until it started to click. He gave C.j the whole clip. He never knew he would see the day he would say R.I.P C.j, and especially not by his hand. He heard his mother's voice saying don't be stupid in his head.

"Ayo Rome quick! Get all this work I'm a go empty the safe upstairs!!" Cash ran upstairs still holding the smoking gun tight in his palm. The two left out the back and without being seen. The safe had $127,000 and 72 ounces of crack. This was the come up of their life. Cash knew he would be making moves on a whole different level now, all thanks to his abusive oldhead C.j.

The streets were buzzing after the death of C.j but nobody knew why or who. The older guys of the block all were catching cases and in and out of jail every few months. Cash and Rome had stepped it up. They hired runners and look outs and acquired shifts to make the block organized. They paid the workers every week, and everything was going smooth. The money was flowing and the block was theirs. Dallas and Cash had gotten back close. They still didn't tell Maria their secret they just wanted to be cool again. He couldn't say no to that pussy, Dallas made sure every time he came over she drained him. She was putting that wet pregnant pussy on him and he loved it. Cash was getting some sloppy wet head from Dallas as they watched Friday on DVD. It was late and he was about to cum. His phone rang and he picked it up.

"Baby I need you to come over we gotta talk." Maria sounded serious so he asked.

"Whats wrong baby?" Dallas knew who it was and still sucked even harder. It felt so good he was about to give his self away. He bit his finger and pushed her head away.

"Just come to my house it's important. What are you doing, you busy?" He took a deep breath as Dallas licked the tip of his dick. He put the phone on mute. "Stop it,stop it,Please!" He told Dallas and took the phone off mute. "Nothing babe I'm on my way ok. I love you." She said I love you more and hung up. "Shit!!!! You be killin that shit what the fuck yo! I gotta go my shorty drawin." Dallas went between his legs and took his whole member in her mouth. She came back up for air and purred.

"You leaving already baby?" He looked down at her with that face and his dick at attention. "In a minute just finish dat!" He grabbed the back of her head and she went to work.

It was an hour later before Cash got over to Maria's house. She was half way sleep when he knocked on her door. She answered and he followed her to her room. He knew he had a problem because he was getting stiff looking at her nice bubble in those lil panties she had on and he was fresh out of some pussy. Maria turned around catching him starring at her booty. "Look baby I don't know what to say I'm pregnant!" That crushed his whole world. He wasn't expecting for her to say that. He still was waiting on his first to be born and now he was having another one. This was just devastating and his kid's mothers were best friends to top it off. Cash started to cry he couldn't hold the lies in any longer it was killing him. Maria looked at her man and was confused with the tears. She never saw this side of Cash he was always so calm and cool. "What's wrong baby? Talk to me!" She held him close wondering why he was so hurt. "I got Dallas pregnant that's my lil boy she having. Baby I'm so sorry!" Cash felt the heavy slaps across his face as Maria began to scream and holler. His face turned red as she went to swing again and he grabbed her by the neck. "You little dick ass nigga you gonna fuck my best friend. Get the fuck out my house. Get out I hate you!!! Get off my neck!" He tossed her on the bed and ripped her panties.

"Stoooop you aint never getting this sweet pussy again nigga! Get off me!" Maria snapped but he held her down.

"Chill baby I'm sorry!" He dove face first and began to do circles with his tongue on her clit. "MMMMMMmmmmmmm!!!" Maria moaned and arched her back as Cash went faster. She thought about her best friend sleeping with her boyfriend as her juices filled Cash's mouth. She grabbed his head and pushed him in deeper as he made his tongue stroke her wet hole. Flashes of Dallas fucking Cash appeared in her head and her body went through spasm. She had never came so hard in her life she squirted and cash gobbled it all up. "Get the fuck out!" she said coldly and curled up in the fetal position. He tried to touch her. "Get out!" He respected her wishes and left without any drama. If he could take it back , he would. This was reality and he had to step up and be a man at a young age and be a father. Now he had lives that were depending on him, he had to turn it up.

Chapter 4

Finding poppy

Months had passed and Maria was still giving Cash the silent treatment. He heard her stomach had been poking out but he didn't see it his self. Him and Dallas had gotten closer but his main objective was to amend his relationship with Maria. With this hustling life cash demeanor changed over awhile. His outer became as hard as his inner. While the game made his heart cold his look was aggressive. He was always strapped because the streets were watching closely. He needed a new connect now that C.j was dead and his work was done he had to find good product for the block. He couldn't just put anything on his block because he never wanted a name for having bad coke. He was on his way to meet up with Rome he said he had some good news and Cash needed to hear that. He had to much money and not enough work. He knew what would happen if he kept that amount of money around it would entice him to buy something expensive. The money he got from C.j he had purchased a few things and put them in the tuck. It was a time and place for everything and he knew Philadephia was a city of hate where he was from and it was far from brotherly love.

Cash knocked on Rome's door and he let him in with a smile on his face. "Yo bull I got some good news."

"Whassup bro?"

"My peoples babymom brother got some fire down south philly he gon look out for us.This nigga saying 7 a O what you tryna do?" Cash shook his head happy to hear he had found a potential connect.

"Whassup with him he cool I aint tryna go to war with these niggas over no money bull. I'm tellin you he burn us it's on you and we gonna go in them niggas. Real shit I'm done taking losses and niggas getting outta line. I just wanna get money!" Cash looked Rome in his eyes he was so serious. He knew this move could change their lives. They would be dealing with someone outside of West Philly, and they didn't even know him. "Look he cool it's my peoples people they not putting me down with no nut. They know I do my thing and said he got it for cheap and I wanted to know how cheap and how good."

"So whassup you leaving me in suspense what is this a horror movie my nigga? Rome laughed. "Naw I copped a few O's and got Jimbo dusty ass in the basement blowin his head off now c'mon." Cash followed Rome in the basement he hadn't seen Jimbo since he sold him that 380. Last thing he heard Jimbo got stomped out down 49th and Thompson for tryna burn this young guy name Rigadel for some coke. Jimbo thought because the kid was 13 he was going to go for $80 in fake money for a 10 for 80 deal. The kid went ham on him and broke 6 of his ribs, the whole hood heard about it.

"Jimbo Jimbo tell me something good, what that work hitting for?" Cash said as he watched Jimbo pull hard on the stem he was smoking from. He blew out the smoke and looked up at Lil Cash from the chair, he had grown since the last time they saw one another. "I told you back then… I saw it in you Lil Cash. You got that look in ya eyes, yeah the streets sucked you right up boy just like they did me." Jimbo took another hit of the stem and Rome and Cash just watched and listened to him speak. "This shit some fire it aint like that last shit but it sure is better then everything around this raggedy motherfucka. It aint been no good coke around this parts since the late 80's. But hey, this some fire for this day and age." Rome looked at Cash who nodded. They were back on.

The next few weeks they were getting the block back in order, Felton street had that work and it spread quickly. Cash made sure all the workers were back focused and everyone would be on point and ready to eat. Cash let Rome deal with the connect. This was his move so he would take whatever loss came from this situation if any. They still split everything 50/50 but Rome was more hands on. He took the money to re up he made that transaction and trip back to the block. It was risky but it was his move so he made sure everything was personally done by him.

Dallas was in nursing school she didn't let her baby stop her education. She wanted more out of life and more for her child. Philly was becoming more and more treacherous and she saw Cash slipping deeper and deeper every day. She tried to talk to Maria but she still was mad. They both had changed so much. Maria was still in school but she began to smoke weed and go out to parties a lot. She was pregnant being on the scene like it was cute. Maria had felt betrayed by her best friend and lover. The weed helped her cope and the parties blocked out her pain even if it was just for a moment.

P.T and D.O.E boy Philly were having a show in the Germantown area of the city. They were local rappers from the city who were young with a buzz and they always brought the ladies out. Maria had never been out that way but her older cousin Dinisha and her girl from around the way Gina was going so she tagged along. Gina was a club hopper and a party girl, she had a reputation of being with every guy who asked for her number. Dinisha was the type that just sat around pretty sipping her drink.

“This party poppin!” Dinisha said to Gina while they stood at the bar waiting for their drinks. Maria heard her song and already was dancing and feeling herself. “Look at Maria shaking her ass with that stomach she know she wrong. Don’t she still fuck wit lil Cash who get money on Felton street?” Dinisha looked at her and rolled her eyes.

”Yeah and stop plottin on my lil cousin baby daddy. You thirsty hoe!”

“Aint nobody thinking about Cash big head ass please!”

“BOC BOC BOC BOC AHHHHHHH!!! Don’t do it!! BOC BOC BOC!!!!” Shots let off and the part was over it was mayhem. Everyone was running in every way to escape and hope they weren’t hit. Bone saw Gina on the floor as people ran by her or stepped on her. He helped her up through all the commotion and ran out with her on his back. Dinisha was out after the first shot, she ran straight to the car and without looking back.. Gina was trying to see who it was and Maria was too high to know what was going on when everyone started running pass her.

Maria looked up and saw black Tae who was reaching for her hand.“I got you c’mon we out!” She grabbed his hand and he guided her out the club.

“Thanks for not runnin me over it was crazy in there and I’m a lil on.” Maria said as she stumbled and smiled.

“C’mon my wheel over here I will take you home. It look like ya people left you.”

Just then Maria realized he was right and she didn’t see her cousin or Gina anywhere. They had left her. “Thank you.” They sat in his car and pulled off. As they rode he told her about hisself. She did the same and they enjoyed each others company. Maria noticed they didn't go far and he pulled up on Kelly drive which was unfamiliar to her as well.

"You tryna smoke?" he said looking down at her stomach seeing that she was pregnant.

"Yeah but don't think you getting no pussy I got a boyfriend. I just need a friend that will be cool, if you not with that drop me off." He looked at her and began to unzip his jeans.

"Look it's cool we good I aint tryna draw I just want some head." Black Tae pulled his penis out which was semi hard. Maria looked down at his darkskin wood and then back up in his eyes.

"Are you fuckin serious? You really gonna pull ya dick out and want some head. I don't even fuckin know you Tae I just met you and I'm gonna suck ya dick with another nigga baby in me? Take me home you outta pocket!!"

Maria was crushed she never wanted to be treated like a whore. She smoked and partied but she never had sex with anyone else. She was mad at Cash but that still was her man. She was just upset with him and chose to cut communication. Her heart was hurt and she felt sick that Tae would disrespect her in such a way. She sat back because she didn't know where she was and had no ride. After he dropped her off this would be the end of their relationship.

Black Tae looked at Maria and put his penis back in his pants. "That's why Cash left ya nutass! Dallas suckin dick bitch you aint!! And you still claiming him like y'all go together. Ayo if you aint sucking no dick get the fuck out my wheel shorty!" Maria sat there stuck he was really talking reckless and trying to kick her out the car. Plus he knew Cash and her business which she didn't like. That really hurt her. "Ohhhh you a deaf bitch you need help to comprehend! I got you baby." He chuckled and got out the car and reappeared on the passenger side. Maria door flew open and with one yank of her arm she was on the ground in the parking lot. Black Tae hopped in his car and mashed off laughing calling her a dumb bitch. She was down Kelly drive by the water at 2 in the morning. She sat there in tears and made the only phone call she could...Cash.

Being as though Maria was clueless to where she was she explained to Cash that She was by the water in a parking lot, a few other cars were down there with people trying to get a late night quickie in. She didn't want to knock on anybody's window and ask for help while they were getting a blow job. So from her description he knew where she could be and finally found her 40 minutes later. Maria got in and Cash didn't wait to ask what happened.

"So what the fuck happened I seen the cops up the jawn I heard somebody got hit at that party?" Maria held her head low in disgust. "What's wrong with you?"

"This nigga pulled his dick out on me. I was at the party and then they start shooting. I didn't know what happened and im high. So he grab me help me out and I peep my bitches left me. So I chilled wit him to get a ride. He pull up here and pull his dick out like suck it suck it." Cash was hot now. He knew the neighborhood knew Maria was his baby's mom. It couldn't of been someone he knew. "Did he touch you? Did he hurt you? What was his name?" Cash asked a thousand questions and wanted a thousand answers. This was his girl and the mother of his child. This was too disrespectful.

"Cash leave it alone don't do nothing to that boy."

"He disrespected my wifey fuck you mean?"

"No you disrespected ya wifey nigga! You fucked my friend and got her pregnant!"

Cash shook his head he was wrong and she was right. "I got to take care of both my kids when they get in this world baby not just one! Yeah I fucked up but I still have to step up and take care of my responsibilities. Why can't you respect it over and we got to get over it and move on. This silent treatment shit call when you in trouble shit is getting corny!" He loved Maria and if he could get her back and this behind them he would do the right by her. Just thinking of her warm tight wetness he began to stiffen as they neared her home.

"Don't even think about it nigga I see ya lil dick getting all hard. This ya baby I'm carrying. Thanks for the ride and being there but you suppose to. So don't get shit twisted!!" Cash got that thought out of his head and they didn't speak the rest of the ride.

When Maria was getting out the car to go inside the house Cash grabbed her arm. "Who ya man?"

She leaned over and kissed his lips. "Thanks for being there I love you boy!" Maria got out and walked inside her home.

The block had been doing good and the customers were responding well to the product and the organization from the block. Rome was buying 9 ounces at a time from his new supplier. He told Cash, for $21,000 that he would sell them a brick. The only thing was they would have to cook it them self. It would be hard powder form. Cash wasn't trying to risk it. He knew the game with them South philly dudes and they was grimy. He didn't want to get reeled in. They could serve you 10 times good work. That

11th time you come through for ten bricks they stick you or you end up missing. Cash was doing every move wisely. "Yo bro get my spot ASAP!!" Rome told Cash sounding upset. They never discussed business over the phone so he wasted no time to get there. Rome was outside already so Cash just pulled up and he got in.

"Whassup nigga?"

"Happy birthday nigga we out!!! Go get Bonez we going to Magic City in Atl." He said excited.

This was how Cash knew the streets had consumed him. He was now 18 and didn't even realize it was his birthday.

"Ayo I can't go nowhere Dallas bout to pop any day now. I gotta be here for that!"

"Look we out for two days c'mon it's ya birthday.She aint bout to pop that jawn out in the next two days." Cash thought about it and said fine. He was ready to ball for once and it was his birthday. He did something many people where he were from didn't…made it to see 18.

They went to scoop up Bonez who had already been to Atl and had a license. They were all in the car contemplating the next move. "Ayo I got to pick my baby up for this trip. Ayo Bonez drive to aunt Queen crib up Darby." Rome was in the back seat rolling a blunt. "Ayo let's just go bull we driving down there we aint got time for stops." Rome said as he perfected the blunt with his lips to finish it. "Yo bull I got dis just chill.Bonez we out." When they got up Aunt Queen 's house it was a little after 11 am. The drive to Atl would take 9 hours. Aunt Queen was a nurse and Cash was her favorite nephew so she let him keep things at her house. Her truck he was paying the note on wasn't in the driveway, so he knew she wasn't home. He had his own key so he was good.

"Cashmoney what we doing here think of all them big booty hoes in Magic city my nigga we wasting time."

"Well we don't need to drive down in this then." Cash hit the remote for the garage and they all saw the black on black Range Rover on 22inch black rims. Rome was impressed and so was Bonez. "Damn Cash this you?" Bonez asked as they all got in.

"I treated myself to something special." Cash said proudly.

Bonez sat behind the wheel and inhaled the new car smell that still lingered. He gripped the wheel and took a deep breath.

"Ayo I think I'm bout to nut this fuckin truck so sexy. We bout to shit on these niggas!" then the trio headed off toward Atl.

The ride wasn't even that long they got to Atlanta around 10:30 that night. They checked into the Holiday Inn. They went to the bar downstairs in the hotel to make a toast to Cash on his birthday.

"To my right hand and my nigga. You the only family I got so I call you my brother. Happy bornday bro lets shit on these niggas and get more paper!" Rome raised his glass and they drank. "Ayo good lookin y'all. Real shit lets go turn it up." Bonez guided the way and they got in the Range and headed toward Magic City. Cash was in the backseat getting his money together that he had on him the rest was in the safe at his room. He wasn't going to an infamous strip club without racks. He had $20,000 on him in hundreds and another 30 in the hotel room. At 18 how could he stop, he was getting money. Real money and it was just the beginning. The parking lot was crazy at Magic city. Rome was already out the window screaming at females. It was ass everywhere. It was more females going in then males.

"Ayo y'all can holla at some real niggas if you want!" Rome hung out the window and reached for the thick short lightskin girl. She was with two friends and it was even more booty. The South was really the ASS nation.

"Where y'all from shawty cuz y'all aint from round herr. We bout to go dance!" The lightskin stallion said and they kept walking slowly. Bonez stayed with them in the Range and Rome tried his hand with the ladies. "We from Philly we in town one night tryna see whats poppin? Me and my niggas tryna bomb aint no rap. Bomb and smoke some bomb!! I know y'all hoes smoke Haze! Fuck dancing what y'all make a night in there be real?" Rome asked feeling his self he had 15 grand on him and another 15 back at the hotel it aint tricking if you got it he thought.

"I make about a1500 a night and its Friday I could get more! If them BMF niggas or any rappers making it rain it's no tellin shawty." The other girl blurted out.

"Whaasup lil shawty y'all payin or what? " The taller one said and Bonez stopped the truck. Cash opened the back door and the three thick country girls piled in. The ladies introduced theselves. Diamond was the short lightskin beauty. Tonja was the thinner brown skin vixen with a thin waist and bubble. Kevalena was the last of the trio and she looked exotic with her green eyes that were cat like. She was 5'5 with flowing shoulder length hair and a nice apple bottom to seduce her customers. She grabbed Cash's hands and admired his tattoos. "I like these shawty…you a bad boy huh?"

"Yeah this me and my nigga Rome right here. Yo Bonez these jawns going back to the tele with us I'm bout to go in on lena!" Cash pulled out his money and starting going through the hundreds. "We aint no broke niggas baby. It's my birthday I'm out here to go hard." All the girls eyed Cash's crisp hundreds as he put it back in his pocket. The girls looked at each other and knew where they were going to tonight, with the Philly guys back to the room.

It wasn't no playing around with these girls they were strickly about their business. The agreement was $1000 a piece for the whole night because they were cool. They were all in there getting it in. Cash had Lena in the bathroom and Rome and Bonez had the other girls on the couch. Sex was in the air of their suite and everyone had a partner and was digging deep. Cash was high as hell he pulled out of kevalena when the door opened up.

"I gotta pee excuse me y'all!!" Tonja came in butt naked and went to the toilet. Cash was in his socks and kevalena was on the floor naked. "What don't stop cuz I'm here aint it ya birthday shawty?"

Cash stood there with his dick throbbing and his head spinning he was drunk and high. He walked over to Tonja on was sitting on the toilet and put his dick in her mouth. "Yeahh you right that's crazzzzzy!" Cash moaned as Tonja went up and down on his pole with her wet full lips. Kevalena crawled over and went to work on his balls. "Oh my fuckin God!" This was not happening he didn't expect both of them he smiled and enjoyed the best moment in his life. The door came flying open again and it was Rome. "DALLAS HAVING THE BABY!!!" He yelled with the phone in his hand butt naked in his boots. Cash turn with the girls still going in on his dick even harder. "Oh shit bull it's her peoples they say she in labor now." Rome said and passed the phone to Cash.

"Hello…ard…im outta town I told dis nigga!" Cash looked down and Lena and Tonja were licking the sides of his dick slowly. "Yeah I be there I'm stuck in Atl. Call my phone when its here and kiss my boy for me." Cash hung up and said to the ladies. "I'ma daddy!!! Now eat dat dick up!!"

The morning came and the sun woke everyone up what was going to be a day of shopping and clubbing would be cut short. Cash was headed back to Philly when everybody was up. His son Cashmere Jahaaz Miller weighed 10.3lbs and was born at 11:30pm February 16, 2005. On his birthday he was had a son and was having the best time of his life. Cash was the first up so he woke everyone and told them be ready to go. He headed downstairs to check out. He left out the room and headed for the elevator. He pressed the button and waited.

The elevator reached his floor and it opened. "Don't fuckin play with me Johnny Where my money?" The guy stabbed the man who was being held by a larger wrestler build Spanish guy. Blood squirted on the floor. Cash couldn't believe his eyes right in front of him.The man with the knife turned around and saw Cash starring. The elevator doors were closing.He put his hand in the way and they opened.

"I aint see shit poppy! It aint my business I don't know bull!" The guy waved for Cash to get on the elevator. He put his hands in the air when he saw the taller guy reach for his gun and the bleeding man fall to the floor. Cash stepped on the elevator and they were going up. “Look I see y'all was doing what y'all was doing I just had a son. I'm from Philly I came here for my birthday I'm 18.”

Cash looked down at the bleeding man on the floor of the elevator and then at the short Mexican with the Knife. He had a scar over his eye that closed his left eye and gave him a scary look. He had a black suit that looked tailored and his hair was in a ponytail. “I knew that accent from somewhere. My cousin from up there the bad lands or something like that,” Cash was shocked the man wasn't coming off threating.

“Yeah that's North Philly I'm from West. I got some peoples up there tho they go hard.”

“I apologize about my associate here.” He wiped the bloody knife on the man's shirt. “He doesn't know how to appreciate a fuckin blessing!!” He kicked the guy in the face busting his mouth. The elevator stopped and the doors open. The husky Spanish guy tucked his gun and walked out and held the door of the elevator. “My name is Face… you look like you tuff, like you a hustler or a gangster. Take my card maybe I can do business with you. This guy down here couldn't get rid of 20 kilos at 10 a piece. You think if I give you that you would fuck it up?”

Cash looked him in the eye and spoke his mind. “You wouldn't be giving me 20 keys I would buy them. So if I fuck that money up it's my money to fuck up not someone else's and I end up on an elevator bleeding.”

Face smirked and looked at Cash with his one good eye that was dark brown but came off as black. Cash took the card and put it in his pocket. “I like that answer…call me I can get to know Philadelphia." Face shook his hand and snatched the weeping man up and walked off with his goon following.

Cash pushed the button for the elevator to close. "Get the fuck outta here…that aint just happen!"

"

Chapter 5

Baby boy

Three months flew by and Cash couldn't believe how much being a daddy he enjoyed. This is what he missed out on as a child, and he promised his son he would be in his life. He let Rome hold it down while he was in daddy mode. Rome and his South Philly connect still were on good business terms. They were flipping half a brick a week. Cash still had that card from Face but he was waiting. He didn't know if he could trust that situation either. He still was waiting for Maria to drop any day now and since the last time he saw her they hadn't spoken. Cash had moved Dallas in a house up the North East area of the city. His mom told him she wanted to move out of Philly, it was becoming too dangerous so he gave her $250,000 and sent her to Florida and Angie came with her. He was slowly making the right moves for his family to better their situation. "Hello…huh?" Cash said as he picked up his cell.

"Get over here now!!" It was Maria and she sounded angry.

"I'm on my way you at the crib?" Cash asked grabbing his keys and heading out the door of his condo on City Ave. "Yeah hurry up!!" Maria hung up and Cash was on the way. When he arrived at her house, he was about to knock and the door swung open. Maria grabbed him and pulled him in. She put her tongue down his throat and they passionately lip locked. Maria was 9 months pregnant and horny as hell she couldn't take it any longer. She wanted to have her baby and get some loving that was long over do. Cash followed her to her bedroom and she laid there on her back with her legs open and her hot pussy purring. Cash came out of his clothes and slowly slid in her dripping vagina. “Daaaammmn baby I miss dis pussy!” Cash moaned as he stroked slow loving every second. Maria had her nails in his arms as he dug deeper with force. “You gonna stop playing and take me back? You don’t miss me? You don’t miss dis dick Maria?” He pounded away at her juicy tightness. “Yes baby I miss you!!! I miss it baby, I MISSSSS IT!!!” She screamed and came all over his dick. “We back together right? Is we back together?!!” Cash thrust harder inside her and looked in her eyes. “Yeah baby yeah we back!! We backkkkkk!” Cash let out a huge nut and rolled over on the bed. “Ahhhhh shit! Damn baby we back together…about time!” Cash laughed and Maria playfully hit him with a closed fist. “I love you Cash but if we back together you gotta stop fuckin Dallas I know that’s ya baby mom now, but that’s my friend and I can’t deal with that shit!” Maria looked him in his eyes and waited for a response.

Cash had been waiting on this moment for months and he wasn’t trying to mess it up. He loved Dallas and she was a rider. His heart was with Maria and if he had to stop he would try as hard as he could for his family. “I’m just going to be there for my son!” He kissed her forehead and she smiled.

Cash wanted to get some fresh air so he hit the block to see how things were going, he hadn’t been in the hood for a while. “What’s poppin out here?” Cash said to one of the runners who was out posted. “Same shit different day chirpin out here as always whassup Cash I heard you quit the game?”

“Naw I just had a lil boy I been staying out the way chillin with my seed.” Cash gets out the car and looks up and down the block the traffic was great it meant money was being made. The blue lights from the Benz shined up the block as it stopped in front of them.

"Yo bull I see you in the hood with it! You aint playing daddy today?" Rome said leaning in his S550. Ever since Rome seen the Range Cash had in the tuck he felt deprived. He wanted to stunt on the haters and show these lames who getting money. Cash still was low key and his truck was parked he only pulled it out for his birthday months ago.

"I don't play daddy nigga! I am daddy!" Cash got in and sunk in the leather of the luxury vehicle.

"Yo bull im fuckin two new bitches everyday on the strength of this jawn. These bitches loving me and the niggas dick eattin crazy. Ayo Rome when you get dat, what year is dat? I'm tellin you pull that Range out bro! We gonna fuck every nigga baby mom in the city!" Rome sounded so excited he was never so happy in his life.

Cash felt his phone vibrate and it was Maria. "Yo...what I'm on the way tell her don't have that baby. I'ma see this one!" He hung up the phone and Rome mashed down on the gas. "She at Penn let's go hurry up!" Cash text Dallas and told her he was on his way to the hospital and meet him there.

Twelve hours later Cash was holding his baby boy in his arms and giving him a kiss. "I love you son!" Casheed Miller was 8.9 lbs and looked just like his daddy. Dallas walked in with little Cash in her arms. She never hated Maria that was her girl. She loved Cash and she couldn't help herself. Maria and Dallas lock eyes foe the first time in 7 months.

"Bitch you had a baby by my man!" Maria snapped.

"Bitch you had a baby by my man!!" They laughed and Maria saw the tears in Dallas eyes. "C'mere girl you know I love you !" Dallas embraced her with a tight hug and the beef was over. Maria looked over at cash who was rocking his son in his arms. “So who it’s gonna be playa? You can’t have ya cake and eat it too?” Dallas chimed in.

“Yeah who is it Cash?” He looked at both his kid’s mother and back at his new born.

“Listen I love both of y’all! I gotta be real I love Dallas, but I’m in love with Maria. So if I had to choose one I would say Maria.”

“Look I’m fine with it I love Cash but if he want you, cool let’s just get us back girl. I miss my bitch. We let dick break us up.”

“Some good dick!” Again they shared a laughed together and they put the drama behind them to move on with their life. Maria picked up lil Cash for the first time and hugged him tight, she saw Cash all in his face.

Chapter 6

The Robbery

Three years flew by and Cash presence in the game was felt and his name was ringing throughout the city. He was labeled as a get money nigga from West by the ladies and a young boss by the competition. If you didn't know him personally you definitely heard of him. Cash had a plan and he was going hard for a reason. He had $200,000 saved for his night club which was his dream business. He was focused and at 21 he was one of the top hustlers in the Tri-State area.

"Yo bull whassup?" Cash walked in Rome's condo that was on the waterfront off of Delaware Ave. Top business people, athletes, actors and A class celebrities resided there. Rome was smoking a dutch in some basketball shorts and socks.

"Take ya shoes off nigga this carpet can't afford no stains my nigga!" Cash smiled and kicked his shoes off and they went into the living room and sat on the leather sectional in front of his 50 inch plasma screen.

Rome put his feet up and explained why he called cash over so early. "Ayo remember the niggas Keith and L?"

"Yeah them dudes ify tho you tryna do business with em?"

"Look they came up in the world cuz I'm at McDonalds with my lil young bitch and I see em. We buss it up L like yo we tryna get with y'all and cop up. Yeah I'm looking at them niggas like yeah ard and kept it pushing. I see these niggas again and L say he wanna cop up and he not playin niggas aint showing love and all this. He pulled out all this money on me."

Cash knew these two since middle school. They were cool and grimy but that's the kind of mentality the guys had in his area and in his city. Cash didn't mind because the streets knew how he and Rome handled problems.He didn't care about serving them the work if it was love, they were from the same area. He wanted everybody to get money and put on for the city. They only get one chance, if they tried anything their next stop would be a grave yard. "How much work they was talking?"

"They want 9 ounces hard!"

"Well let's make it happen tell em meet us on Robinson street. Any funny business I'm airing niggas from the rip." Rome shook his head in agreement and made the call.

$ $ $ $ $ $ $ $ $ $ $ $ $ $ $ $ $

"Ayo L, who the fuck told you to get work from these clowns?"

"I told you they got oils and they know us so they gonna look out. Chill bull I got this." L said confidently. He was ready to eat and get real money, and dealing with Cash would certainly upgrade them.

"Man fuck them niggas! I remember when Anthony, fuck a Cash was sellin candy nigga! That shit better be official or I'm offin these niggas.Real rap dog I keep hearing this nigga Cash name every where, I'm getting sick of it. My bitch know him and my babymom. Them bitches dick eat like he a rapper or some shit!" Keith snapped. He was a pure hater but it was never in your face it was behind your back. He envied Cash's position and only time would tell how their worlds would collide. Cash never knew why he felt this way he always spoke when he saw him and they knew each other for years.

When L pulled up on Robinson Street he called Rome for the address. "Yo bull we out here what's the address?" Cash played it smart he had Stash houses all over the city. This particular spot on Robinson was just a safe house. This is where they met new customers and if things didn't look right that's where they left them, wrapped up and in the basement. Then they would move to another spot. Rome hoped it didn't come to that and it was just business, he told them the address then waited.

"Ayo chill the fuck out Keith when we get in here niggas aint the same as they was in middle school. Niggas grown men and I wanna get bread!"

"Just come on fuck these niggas tho!" L and Keith walked to the door and Rome let them in. Rome was smoking a Dutch with the work on the table and Cash was just standing there with the Mac 10. Keith looked at the high powered weapon Cash was holding and smirked. "Whassup Anthony?" No one called Cash by his government and he felt disrespected because he knew Keith was aware of that. "Who the fuck you callin Anthony bull? My name Cash! You know my name nigga. Ayo Rome pat these niggas down." Rome did as Cash instructed and L was clean but Keith had a 22 in his back pocket. "My bad Cash I just want that fire heard you had the best coke around here." Keith said raising his hands in the air.

"Yo bull stop talking so damn hot what you wired or something nigga. Chill the fuck out, get ya shit and roll this a real simple procedure. Where the money at?"

"I got you right here!" L pulled the wad of money from his pants.

"Here you go Cash $7500!" L said proudly and placed it on the table. Rome scooped it up and passed the work off as he counted.

"That money good playboy you aint gotta count it!" Keith blurted out.

"Solid... well we done here boys y'all have a good one." Cash opened the door and held the Mac 10 close. Their new customers left without any problems.

$ $ $ $ $ $ $ $ $ $ $ $ $ $ $ $ $

On his way to Maria's house Cash stopped by the Chinese store to get a Dutch. He watched the young girl at the counter with the long hair and petite frame order her food. She was cute but Cash could tell she was a young buck. "You bout to get them cat wings huh?" The girl turned around and looked Cash up and down. She zoomed in on his wrist that glistened from the Iced out presidential Rolex. None of the hustlers around her way had that. She saw the tats on his hands and seen Cash. Even the young girl had heard about him.

"Yeah I'm getting them why you actin like you going to take me out to eat or something." The pretty young lady spat back.

"I might you never know if you play ya part right. C'mon we out let me drop you off at ya house!"

"I only live up the street I'm cool I don't know you!" She lied and bit her bottom lip as she eyed Cash and his watch.

"Well get to know me I got a lil check for you!" She looked at him in his eyes with a smile. "Ard!"

They got in Cash's car and he learned she was 17 about to be 18 in a few months. She lived with her mom on 45th street and had a boyfriend who wasn't holding it down at all. After the small talk she agreed to chill with him for a few. Cash was on a time schedule but this was new pussy so he drove to the Blue Moon.

"Ewwww this room nasty!" Wydia said as her and Cash came into the small room with a bed and sink. The Blue Moon was infamous in West Philly, it had been around for years. The only problem was it was usually occupied by the local crack heads and their tricks. Cash didn't care about that he just wanted to hit this young pussy real quick.

"We aint got time to play with it." Cash pulled out his dick and sat down on the bed. "C'mere!" He grabbed Wydia's hand and she went to her knees. "Young bitches don't really suck dick dat good…you different?" Wydia didn't speak she opened her mouth wide and devoured his penis. "Hmmmmmmmm….."

After the great head and some good tight pussy, Cash put $150 in her pocket and dropped her off. When he came in the house Maria was in the bedroom lying down with his son watching cartoons. He looked at Maria who had a slight attitude. "Whats wrong with you?" He said getting his towel and wash cloth ready to shower and call it a night.

"You get Dallas pussy juices off ya dick!!?" she barked at him.

"Baby I'm tired and I didn't fuck Dallas that's on my kids. Now can I wash my ass I been in the streets all day." Cash left her there and she dialed Dallas cell when he gort in the shower.

"A girl did you just fuck Cash today?"

"Huh Maria I been at school, I just picked the baby up from the sitter what's wrong he came in smelling like pussy?"

"You know how that woman intuition kick in. My shit tingling I know he was fucking somebody I aint stupid. But ard girl bring my baby over on the weekend."

When Cash emerged from the bathroom his son was sleep. Maria had put him in his crib. Cash still was dripping water from his bodyand walked over to Maria and pulled the covers back. She was naked and he caught her off guard.

"I know what you need!!!" He smacked her on the ass and dove between her cheeks face first from the back.

$ $ $ $ $ $ $ $ $ $ $ $ $ $ $ $ $

L and Keith had been making moves on 49th and Kershaw with the work they got from Cash. The fiends were calling constantly and they were making real money. They both sat in the trap house they had bagging up the last ounce. "Ayo L you tryna come up and get even more paper nigga?" Keith said like he had the master plan.

"Nigga I'm all about coming up what you got on ya mind bull?"

"I'm talking about jammin Cash and Rome. It's been two months since we been coppin up faithfully! Them niggas not expecting it. Cash stay with 10 racks on him and Rome got a Benz, nigga we on!" L just shook his head. This was his right hand man so for so many years they were tight. He was tripping L thought, this was the first time in his life he was seeing real money. He wasn't about to risk his life and his pockets.Keith continued to explain how it would work and L responded with why it was stupid. This was Keith's come up and he was tired of bleeding the block...he wanted more. Keith ignored him and made the call to re up.

"Hello, same chicken platter, I'll be there in 15 minutes." L said to Rome to let him know he was getting the same work as before, 9 ounces.

"I'm telling you this gonna work I pull out on Cash pop him from the rip Rome give us the shit we pop him then we good!" Keith was ready to do Cash in and it wasn't because he wanted his money. His insides were filled with hate and they came from the same era. He wondered why Cash was up and he was still scrambling. L wasn't with it at all but Keith was his man and his mind was made up. "Get the burners!" Keith ordered and L went to the stash in the basement where they kept the guns.

"This some bull shit! This nigga giving us a death sentence." L said and held the guns in his hand. He shook his head and said fuck it! It was now or never.

L was sweating bullets and Keith had a smirk on his face as they walked through the door s and was greeted by Cash and Rome. L heart was beating so hard and fast he thought Cash seen it through his shirt.

"So whassup y'all ready or y'all just gonna stand there looking all nervous. Yo bull you good L you don't look so good?" Cash said and L looked at Keith.

"Fuck dat shit! Give us all the work and the money!" Keith whipped out his gun and caught Cash off guard as well as Rome. Cash and Rome had got comfortable and didn't have their guns out but they both were strapped. Keith looked at L who was frozen he hadn't pulled his gun out yet. "Yo bull get the money. Whassup with you we did it we good! Fuck this nigga!" He yelled and put the gun to Cash's face. He walked up closer and Cash could smell the weed on his breath. "So Anthony how much money you got for me?" He mushed the gun in his face and pulled the trigger.

CLICK CLICK CLICK CLICK the sound of the empty gun engulfed Keith with fear.

"Pussy!!" Cash punched him in the face hard knocking him to the floor. Then L pulled his gun and let off a shot. BOC !!!

Keith eyes widen as the bullet penetrated his chest. Cash and Rome both were confused. L stood with the smoking gun in hand and teary eyes. This was his friend on the floor bleeding. He didn't want it to come to this but he wasn't as greedy as Keith or as stupid. "I told you nigga let's get money.You wanna draw and fuck my situation up. Stupid, you stupid nigga!" Keith felt the blood pouring from his chest and his life flashed before his eyes. He reached in his back pocket with his last bit of strength and L never seen it coming. POP POP!! He fired two shots at L's head with the 22 in his back pocket. L slumped over lifeless and Keith let out his last breath.

"That's crazy I told you don't fuck with these niggas" Cash stepped over the dead bodies and he and Rome fled the scene.

Chapter 7

That SHIT

Maria and Dallas had overcome something that made their friendship even tighter. The same baby father was weird for a minute until they really saw the fruits of it. Cash was taking care of both families. They didn't want for nothing. Dallas had an X5 BMW as well as Maria, they were getting money so the people could say whatever they wanted. They didn't care because they were good.

"Where you going yo?" Cash asked Maria as she was getting dressed to go out clubbing with her girls.

"To Palmers why whassup baby you gonna pop up on me stalker?" Maria laughed and looked at her slim waist and round ass in that Black Vera Wang dress. Having her child made her hips spread and her hair grow. She was killing them softly physically. "I just need to know where my wifey gonna be at. You know niggas pull dicks out on you!" Cash joked and Maria punched him twice.

"Shut up Cash I still remember that shit! The honking outside of a horn made Cash looked out the window. BEEEP BEEEP!!!

"What the fuck? Ohhhh hell naw... not in my shit y'all not!" Cash saw Dallas outside in his Range Rover that he still never drove around the city. Rome was stunting enough for the both of them with the attention from the Benz. "Well tell Dallas that." Maria said knowing Cash was weak and never told her no. Since she played her part with the Maria situation he just said yes to everything, plus she was still sucking his dick every here and there on the low. "Just go head its cool fuck it I'm a call Rome." Maria kissed his lips and was out the door. Cash quickly grabbed his cell and dialed Rome. "Yo bull where we at tonight?"

"The streets say Palmers gonna be off the chain. You know them niggas got signed they having they party there!"

"Who?"

"P.T and D.O.E boy Philly signed with Def Jam."

"Oh that's whassup, P.T my nigga! We out pick me up in a hour!" Cash wasn't getting too fly he and the rest of the city knew he was good. He put some Evisu jeans on, white t shirt wth the Louis Vuitton belt and matching chucks. He knew since it was a rapper's party the cameras would be out. He was going to wear his chain for the first time tonight he got a couple months back made by his jeweler. He went in his walk in closet and grabbed a black fitted with the grey P. When he stood in the mirror he placed his ice on. The Rolex was already blinging and the chain was retarded. It was a diamond infested chain with the W.P piece flooded with yellow diamonds. Rome pulled up and Cash grabbed 20 racks out the safe all fresh bills the long way and they were headed to stunt.

"Damn nigga you stay poppin up with some shit!" Cash looked at Rome who had a red Phillies hat, white polo thermal, red green and white Gucci belt, and the matching Gucci sneakers. Rome had an iced out Breitling and his Jesus piece was flooded with yellow diamonds. They were from West Philly it came natural to them to dress. Rome lifted Cash's piece in his hand and it was heavy.

"Yeah this jawn right I need to wear that! We bout to kill these niggas!" Cash leaned his seat back and rolled up a Dutch for the ride. They picked up Bonez who told them he was doing a verse on P.T's song tonight at Palmers and they were doing a video. Cash saw in his face he was hype and this meant a lot to him.

"You better rip that shit bull you gonna be in a video, you gotta stunt!" Bonez looked down at hisself as if he wasn't fresh to death. He had a Bathing Ape sweat suit on, with the matching sneakers.

"Naw I see you nigga, you fly but you need dis. Here!" Cash took of his chain and put it around his cousin's neck. Bonez shook his head appreciative but happy and gave him a hand shake.

"Yeah I'm gonna fuck shit up tonight!"

They got to Palmers and it was packed the line was around the block. The whole city was in there tonight. "Ayo pull up in the front Rome I'm performing and we looking like a million we good.Y'all don't believe me I got a lil buzz with this rap shit." They pulled up in the front like real celebritys.

"Whoa you can't." The husky security guard with the tight tshirt said but looked in the car and saw Bonez. "Oh whassup bro I got ya passes for V.I.P, The BAU team already in there." He passed them their V.I.P passes and they stepped out the car like stars. Girls were pointing and whispering inquiring to the next who were the guys in the Benz all icey.

"Hey Cash!" He looked back and didn't notice who the light skin girl with big breast was. "Hold up y'all…do I know you?"

"It's me Dinisha Maria peoples." Bonez walked over and she smiled and eyed his chain.Cash thought he heard that name before and it clicked. "Ohhhh you the jawn that left Maria at the party when they start choppin."He laughed and just walked off.

"Ayo whassup with ya girl Gina?" Bonez remembered she was a freak and had some good pussy. She rolled her eyes. "Ewwww you checkin for dat?"

"Why you say dat?"

"She got that shit! Niggas lookin for her, they on her top!!! She gave 6 niggas Aids. They ran a train on her after Meek Mill show a couple months ago." Bonez stomach curled and he felt like he was about to shit on his self. Rome pulled his arm and they all went in the club. As the spot light hit them Bonez couldn't enjoy it. His mind was on when did Gina get it and was it before or after him. "Ayo there go ya babymomma's!" Rome said pointing to Dallas in Maria at the bar. Cash gave them a head nod and whispered in Bonez ear. "Yo cuz you cool? You lookin funny."

"Yeah I just got to take a shit I be back y'all get some bottles let me hit the bathroom." Bonez sped off through the thick crowd and Rome and Cash headed toward V.I.P.

P.T greeted them with a bottle of Henny in his hand.

"Congrates bull I heard you got signed. Put on for the city!!" Cash said in his ear over the loud music. Philly was filled with rappers and he was proud a real nigga from the city was on that deserved it. The cameras flashed and Cash, Rome ,and P.T posed for a picture while bonez stressed in the bathroom.

“Please God not me! Please God not me, let me be straight. Don’t let this bitch give me Aids!!” Bonez said as he looked his self in the mirror and tossed some water on his face. This was his night to shine and stunt for West Philly. It took all of him to put this deep in his mind and enjoy the night, but the weed and liquor would help.

$ $ $ $ $ $ $ $ $ $ $ $ $ $ $ $ $

The next morning Cash woke up to a crazy hangover on the hotel floor. The last thing he remembered was ordering 20 bottles of Rose when they started recording the video. Bonez was ripping the track with so much passion he thought he was about to cry. He got up and Bone was fully clothed on the couch smoking a cigarette teary eyed.

“What the fuck wrong with you cuz?” Bonez just sat there and broke out crying. “That bitch Gina got that shit and I fucked her raw. I use to bomb that all crazy! I’m fucked she out here torching niggas Dinisha said niggas was lookin for her! Yo cuz I can’t live if I got dat shit. I love pussy too much.” Cash knew something was wrong and he was hurting for his cousin. If he had the Aids it was like Gina killed him.

“Yo cuz just go to the doctor and see for yaself fuck thinking about it. Know ya status. Atleast know for sure you aint fucked shorty since when?”

“It’s been a minute.”

“Well get tested stop playing!”

$ $ $ $ $ $ $ $ $ $ $ $ $ $ $ $ $ $

It had been a week since Bonez had taken his test he came back for his results and was so nervous. He waited in the Doctor's office for 5 long minutes before he came back in with a folder. "Yes Mr Bryan Miller?" The doctor asked.

"Yeah what's the verdict I need to know fuck that it's been a week!" Bonez snapped.

The elder white man shook his head and placed his hand on Bonez shoulder.

"Calm down young man I'm just the messenger. I'm sorry you have tested positive for HIV."

"So I don't have Aids?"

"No you have H.I.V,not full blown Aids. You can still live a strong life if you take your medicine and---------

"SHUT THE FUCK UP!!!! I still got that shit...I'm dead!" Bonez dropped to the floor in tears. All the women in his past, they flashed across his mind vividly. Then Gina's face appeared and she was laughing at him.

"Stop laughing at me stop laughing!!! I hate you!!!Stop laughing!!!" He screamed and the old white man got spooked. The doctor left him in his office to let out his frustration. Bonez was now another statistic, a young black man with HIV.

Chapter 8

Relocate

“Ayo we got problems!!” Rome had bad news and just when everything was smooth something always come up. The deeper cash got into the drug game the farther his dreams of being a club owner went. He was still saving and had over $300,000 just for that. Every time beef or a money problem arose Cash thought of the club and how it couldn’t have this much headache in running it.

“What now my nigga?” Cash said as Rome slammed the door to his condo and sat down on the couch. “My connect from South Philly got popped!” Cash shook his head, this was bad. “How much work you get last from him?”

“4 bricks!”

“Damn bull I hope they not watching him and watched you. The Feds or locals?”

“The Feds they hit his spot 5 in the morning it was on the news. They found 10 birds, 50lbs of weed, two choppers and some handguns. Shit not looking good!”

“That’s crazy! What the fuck he know, if he flip he can use against us? You know these niggas rats out here. Cream from North Philly who use to be getting all that paper remember bull. He told on his right hand man Sin and got him 15 years! These niggas aint playing fair.”

“We good he doesn’t know shit bout you or our shit. I did show him the block a long time ago to show him how his coke was moving out in West. That’s about it.” Cash looked at his long time friend and just shook his head. “C’mon Rome what if the nigga start tellin he gonna have our shit hot! That nigga facing forever and a day he might crack! Plus you prolly was watched when you went to go cop. Shut Felton down bull. Nothing gets sold on that block, NOTHING!" He stood up and started pacing back and forth thinking of his new move.

"Look I can holla at Fat Mike and get some work on Lansdowne Ave you know he runnin that shitfrom 59th to 63rd. Plus see whassup with my nigga J-Jay and put some work on 49thThompson. Rome we gotta switch up, if we hot, we getting locked the fuck up. Hit them streets lets relocate!"

"My fault bro I fucked up I should have did shit different!"

"Ayo fuck dat shit. I'm really ready to get this club poppin.You know Atl hot right now I'm bout to do this shit! We just gotta leave the game alone.You think you can go legit after all this?"

"I don't know bro I don't know!" Rome gave him a shake and headed toward the door.

"Yo bull...park that Benz too. We hot, that just bring more attention. Hop back in the squader for a lil bit until shit die down." Rome nodded his head and went to handle business. Cash wasn't taking any chances.He didn't trust the situation, or the connect and getting popped after Rome copped up. Plus he knew what block they were moving work on, it was just too much against them. He dialed his homie Fat Mike.

"Yo bull whassup wit you?"

"I need a favor. Meet me down 69th street the new 50cent shit coming out tonight!"

"What time?"

"7, I be at McDonalds." Fat Mike thought to hisself for a minute. The 50cent moving came out a last year, so this had to be business and he wanted to sit down and eat together, and not McDonalds. Cash was his friend since the school days when he actually went. He knew he was getting serious money now so he was with discussing business. "I see you there."

They hung up and Cash was in the mood for some pussy. He looked through his phone and saw who it was it going to be from the missed call, Wydia! Cash dialed her number and realized it was a couple months since he hit but she was always calling or texting telling him come get it and how much her boyfriend in the way.

"Hello?"

"You busy or I can get some time in?"

"Who dis Cash? I'm chillin where you at, come get me!!! I'm bored!"

"Be there in a minute."

"Hurry up before my dude get back." Cash chuckled lightly and hung up the phone. Cash pulled up around 45th street 15 minutes later. A few guys in white t-shirts polluted the corner. This area was full of hood rats and street level dealers but they had some flowers in the concrete such as Wydia. She was on the steps with two girls one was darkskin and the other was chubby and brownskin. Three guys were playing dice in front of her house for a few bucks.

"We out c'mon I got moves to make lil butt!" Wydia smiled and told her cousins she would be right back. The kid on the dice who couldn't be older then 19 in an oversized white t shirt spoke up.

"Damn Wydia you outta pocket!"

"What? Mind ya business!!!" She snapped with attitude.

Just as Wydia was getting in the car her boyfriend appeared from around the corner with grocery bags. "Shit!" Wydia quickly got in the car.

"Ayo D look at ya girl bull." The young guy said. Cash looked in his mirror and put the gun on his lap so he could see it if he acted up.

"Just pull off Cash I don't feel like hearin this shit. Let's go." Cash was just about to put the car in drive before her boyfriend's face was at his window.

"Whoa whoa who dis babe?"

"It's my cousin Cash baby we bout to go see my Aunt real quick she having something on 49th street. I be right back." Wydia 's face was so serious her boyfriend looked at Cash then back at her. "Babe this ya cousin?" She shook her head back and forth.

"YEEESSS I just said that." He finally looked on Cash's lap and saw the pistol. He looked back at the guys behind him that were playing dice.

"Yo bull that's Cash, oh shit yeah fallback that prolly is her cousin I thought she was fuckin. She not gonna just have a nigga come to the crib like dat." The guy said but he didn't really believe it. He just heard about Rome and Cash and wasn't trying to have that problem.

"For real?" He dropped the bags and swung on Cash who was still sitting in the car listening as the kid defended him. It must of clicked in his head who he was and Cash smiled. That's when he felt the wind go across his face and the guy fist hit his horn. HONK!!

"This nigga just swung on me?" Cash pushed the door open and it hit David's stomach hard backing him up. Cash grabbed the gun and was about to get out. The three kids that were playing dice ran down the block when they saw him getting out. Wydia grabbed his arm.

"NOOOOO don't do it CASH NOO!!!!" Cash yanked his arm away and quickly swung the gun across David's face opening his cheek up. "Arrrggghhhh!!" He hit the ground holding his face. Cash stood over him pointing the gun enraged at how disrespectful and bold he was. You don't ever get mad at the guy when your girl cheating. He doing what any man would do, get the pussy.

"Yo bull is you fuckin crazy? I should off ya nut ass right now for that nut shit. Get up!!" Cash ordered and the guy stood up still holding his leaking face. Cash tucked the gun as the staggering boyfriend stood wobbling. He got close and hit him with a vicious uppercut knocking him out cold.

"Yo get ya shit together shorty you got me out here knockin niggas the fuck out I'm suppose to be knockin down some pussy. Hit me when you single or something."

Cash pulled his pants up on his waist and left her trying to wake up her boyfriend on the curb.

7:00 came quick, Cash thought to himself it really wasn't enough hours in a day. He was waiting in McDonalds parking lot and heard the loud system of the 2004 Escalade Fat Mike was in. Cash got out his car and hopped in the truck. Fat Mike noticed the print from Cash's gun under his shirt and thought about his that was under the seat.

"My nigga Mike whassup with you bull? I'm getting right to it whats the move with the Ave?"

"What you mean Felton do numbers what you want with the Ave?"

"Look I'm shutting the block down for a minute I want to expand." Fat Mike shook his head but he wanted to know numbers how was this benefiting him.

"So what I get?"

"Everbody know my block do numbers, real shit it do triple the whole Ave. But the Ave is the Ave and that's one block. I put my workers out here we go by my set up tho. We organize shit so money straight and the customers happy and loyal. I ain't come on no goon shit cuz I fuck with you! I got plans, and this the money train nigga! Whassup 50/50 split on the month's gross?" Fat Mike thought about how Cash transformed Felton to a million dollar block. He had the Ave on smash and it only did a couple hundred thousand. Millions or hundreds of thousands?

"I'm with it let me know bull!" They shook hands and Cash's plan was coming together. Now it was time to make a call that he thought about every day since he met him. He needed Face for that out of town work. He knew Mexicans were about they business and always had the best quality. At ten a key how could he lose?

"Hello can I speak to Face this is Cash?"

The phone was silent and then the deep tone Spanish accent came on the line.

"Mr. Cash it's been a long time I thought you were dead...you know your kind are very dangerous."

"As well as yours...we both witnessed that."

"Right!"

"Look I heard your pit bull had puppies. I'll be in town Friday if there still some around I will need 10. They love them pure breeds up here so I will re- sell them for a good profit. As long as the price still cheap?" Face started to laugh an evil like giggle. He respected Cash's secret way of saying 10 bricks if they still 10 a piece like he said.

"Yes I do have some left, my red nose just had 16 puppies so you are fine. Mr. Cash I don't want to see anybody but you ok?" It got quiet before he spoke.

"I just wanna see you!" Cash replied.

"I wouldn't have it no other way my friend. I will have my private plane pick you up so you can get here faster. Just make sure your money is straight."

"My money always straight, see you Friday!"

It was time to get that real money. As a drug dealer, you hope to reach a certain status when you deal with a real connect that has it in. This can change lives and Cash knew it , he was on his way to the top with this alliance. He broke every thing down with Rome and he was just as excited about the new connect. Rome was ready to snap when Cash told him in Atlanta the Mexican made him get on the elevator and he stabbed some guy in front of him. Cash told him he gave him a card and said 10 a key and Rome was like that was gangster.

Rome gave up 50 thousand and Cash put up the other. Cash put everything in the Gucci duffel bag and was ready to go.

"Yo bull after we get done this and this shit official we grabbing heavy. We test the waters first with 10." Cash gave his homie a shake and left to catch a plane. It was time to turn up for real.

Face gave him instructions to go to the clear port and his Private jet would be waiting. He couldn't believe the trip, he had champagne and Face had two Spanish ladies in their birthday suits and red bottoms perform a good show.

The plane landed 2 hrs later in a farm like area on the outside of Atlanta. Cash stepped off the plane and Face stood there leaning against a cherry red candy apple 745 Bmw. Cash stepped off and checked the surroundings. Nothing was out here but land and barns.

"Ayo Face you got me in the sticks you know I'm a city slicker." They shook hands and Cash looked in his one dark eye that seemed black. Face was spooky and had a scary movie villain look about him.

"There are no problems out here Mr. Cash.This is all my land. When you obtain a certain level of success in whatever you do you can spend your money wisely."

"So you buy a plane and a farm?" They laughed and Face took him to see what he came for. They got to the barn and hopped out. Cash put the money on the hood of the car.

"100 grand right here poppy! If this shit pop like I think it should, I want 50 next time." He said confidently. Face walked over to a refrigerator that was in the corner. He opened it and pulled out a black duffel bag. He brought the bag over to his car and put it on the hood also. He unzipped it and there they were wrapped neatly in plastic. Face popped his knife out and cut one down the middle. "Try some." Face said and snorted some coke off the knife and passed it to Cash.

"Let me see dis shit." He took the knife and got some more powder from the brick. He snorted it and his nose burned. He got light headed and his face was numb. This was his first time ever doing cocaine but he couldn't turn this opportunity down. If Face needed him to test it he thought maybe that would show he was official.

"Yeah we good that shit got my face numb and I don't even fuck around. So how we getting it back?"

"You did your job you paid the money. Write down the address and I will have it sent by tomorrow." Face had been distributing drugs over 15 years in over 20 states and 50 cities. His reign on the top was far from over.

Cash just thought this was even better, he didn't have to take the risk of bringing it back. He wrote down the address to one of his stash houses and tried to shake the high off. That one snort had him seeing double for a second. "You okay Mr. Cash?"

"Yeah that shit got me super high. How the fuck people just snort all day… shit!"

“You get back on the plane and go home, enjoy the ladies and relax. I’m going to make you a very wealthy man…are you ready for real power?”

“I always told people since I was a young nigga, not knowing shit about the game. I wanna be the boss…I like runnin shit…I’m a boss! So I’m ready I was born ready!”

Chapter 9

They Watching

The only problem Cash was havinglately, was where to put all his money. The first ten flew like hot cakes on the block. Lansdowne Ave was doing numbers and the organized alliance he and Fat Mike peoples had was great. 49th and Thompson to 52nd was on lock. Cash gave J-Jay the same deal as Fat Mike. He was making million dollar moves and connecting with the right people, putting together a takeover of neighborhoods that distributed drugs but also provided for the families by buying their homes. No one complained when he showed up to their door with a bag full of hundreds. Cash's name spread he flew to another level in the game quick. The streets were watching.

"Hello can I speak with Mr. Treveani?"

"Hold please," the young woman said politely.

"Mr. Treveani speaking how may I help you?"

"Yes this is Anthony Miller I want to know were those blueprints ready we went over? For my club." Mr. Treveani was the lawyer Cash hired. He had a contractor ready and the club was in the process of being built after a couple more signatures. Cash gave his lawyer a down payment of $500,000, he needed everything legit.

"Yes Mr. Miller last time we talked I was on that, and they are done. I need the name so we can get that paper work drawn up as well."

"Faith I' m going with Club Faith, A perfect Lounge. That shit sound hot I paid you so keep me informed I have another 500 by the end of the week!"

"Great but could you do me a favor, try not to bring all that money to my office like last time. That didn't look right?"

"You the lawyer I can meet you somewhere else but all I got is cash. I can't write a check stop acting like you don't know my situation." Click

$ $ $ $ $ $ $ $ $ $ $ $ $ $ $ $ $

Rome was at a red light when he checked his rear view and noticed the unmarked cop cars speeding his way. He hit the stash box and tossed his 40 cal in and shut it. Just as he thought they surrounded him and hopped out yelling FREEZE.

"Get out the fuckin car asshole before I think you reaching!!" He looked around and these were Feds. He put his hands out the window and they moved in.

"What I do man? I haven't broken the law why you putting cuffs on me?" Rome yelled and an agent got in his car and pulled off. Guns were drawn on him until he was in the back of the Tahoe that pulled up. Rome cell vibrated he was on his way to meet Cash he knew that was him.

"What the fuck I do?" He sat cuffed in the back of the truck in between two white men with their guns out.

"So you're Mr.Jerome Davis! Or should I say Rome? Your big time now huh? I'm Special Agent Galvin I know a lot about you already. My South Philly informant let us know a whole lot about you. Then we start watching because we can't just go off him, because I never heard of you guys.I thought he was pulling my leg"

Rome looked at him and wondered what he meant by you guys? Then he kept talking and Rome listened carefully without saying a word.

"I know about Felton Street. Your butt buddy Cash! I want info on him, who he buying from I want you to set up a buy. Or we can look deep into a few bodies that came up missing a while back. L and Keith!! I know you guys were selling them heavy weight because my other Ace in the hole told me that one. Now fuck with me and don't cooperate you will be Moses age when you get out of federal prison. I hate drug dealers. Get a fucking job."

Rome couldn't believe it, his South Philly connect was ratting. It just weren't any real niggas left in the game.

"I'm sorry sir but I need to speak with my lawyer or you can let me go." Rome looked at the pale faces that starred him down.

"Or you can suck my dick!!" Agent Galvin and his partner began to beat his ribs with their guns.

"Arrrrgggghhhh what the fuck y'all doing!!" Rome screamed and Agent Galvin went in his pockets and removed his money and cell.

"Look you save yourself now or when we do get you motherfuckers, which is very soon. You fry! Because when we really come we got all we need asshole!" The car abruptly stopped and they uncuffed him.

"Get the fuck out?" They had Rome on the side of the road looking dumbfounded.

"Yo bull where my car at?" He yelled as they were about to close the door.

"Consider it a gift for my son. You look better in the Benz." Then they peeled off leaving him on the side of the road with no money or cellphone.

$ $ $ $ $ $ $ $ $ $ $ $ $ $ $ $ $ $

Cash had been calling Rome all day his phone was off. Something was wrong and he knew it, they were suppose to meet hours ago. Cash was at his Condo snapping with his gun in his hand. If anyone touched his best friend it would be bloodshed. Knocks at his door took him from his daze.

"Who is it?" He looked through the peephole and saw it was Rome, he quickly opened the door.

"Nigga where the fuck you been at?" Cash barked. Rome came in with the, we got a problem look. When Rome told Cash what happened he couldn't believe it. How did they know so much? Why did they let Rome go if they had so much information? They had nothing solid and Cash wasn't trying to give them anything. Why did they want him so bad though, he was one of the largest drug dealers in the city but he was low key. He didn't throw it in their face with fancy cars and throwing money, all he did was stack and feed his family and plenty of others. He hated rats and that's the reason they knew anything. NIGGAS RUNNING THEY MOUTH!!!

"Look I say let's get the fuck outta here before they build a strong enough case to book us! Let's go to Atlanta and wait this club thing out. I like this lifestyle bro fuck going to jail, we up!" Cash listened to his life long friend and understood where he was coming from, but he wasn't done yet. He had money to get and the plug was blessing him.

"Rome I can't just up and leave, I got kids and a family. I'm leaving but not right now not this week or next month!"

"So what you saying Cash? We hot!"

"We not hot hot. If they had something real you would still be locked up. Believe that bro.Its time for us to just go hard on these niggas and then roll out caked up. The connect giving them 10 a jawn! 10!! This shit don't come easy bull and I aint giving it up yet."

"You my nigga Cash…I'm riding with you bro! What you got planned?"

"Operation takeover!"

Operation Takeover was some Mafia type shit. The only way it would work is if they had legal and powerful representation. If they didn't have someone in their pocket of power in the city it wouldn't work. So he made a phone call.

$ $ $ $ $ $ $ $ $ $ $ $ $ $ $ $ $

"Hurry out the bathroom girl, daddy ready!" The Mayor of the city was in a motel room in a secluded area in the city with a nice young thick ebony goddess. He was tied to the bed blindfolded and she was changing in the bathroom to turn on her dominatrix swagger. The Mayor had some kinky fantasies and Juicy was there to fulfill them. She was 6 feet tall 180lbs.She was all ass, titties, thighs and hips. Her stomach was flat with a slight 4 pack. Her ebony skin was smooth and she had tiger stripes on the side of her body tattooed that gave her that extra sexiness.

“WHAT THE FUCK YOU SAY MOTHERFUCKER!?” She yelled coming out the bathroom and setting up the camcorder on top of the T.V. She was in a leather cat suit and clutched a black whip. Juicy was a stripper from West Philly, and when Cash said he needed a favor she was on it. She was always with a come up. After a half hour of smacking her victims back and backside the door of the motel opened. Cash and Rome came in smiling at the freaky Mayor of Philadelphia tied up getting a spanking.

“Who dat? Ay baby girl who is that?” Cash lifted his blindfold and the Mayor was scared to death, he was set up.

“What is this all about?” He said still tied up.

“I need your help bro and it looks like you could use mine!”

“Why would I need help from you? Your just some young punk!”

“Okay okay we calling names. How about the media get your sex type I wonder what that would do to your campaign and the city of brotherly love. What if I youtube this shit?” Rome showed the Mayor his video and his eyes grew wide.

“You black mailing me?”

“We doing business! You gonna get paid so it aint blackmail. This is what I need from you. Protection and for your cops to look the other way on a few areas I do business at. My team that I’m putting together I need for them to get a stay out of jail free card, if there in my organization. I will pay you 100,000 a month for as long as we in business. If you can't do this for me I think you might have a debut on youtube." Cash tossed a bag of money on the floor which was his first payment .

"That's a100 racks bull I will be in touch." Cash and Rome left and the main part to Cash's Takeover was out the way.

What started like mission impossible became easy once they had the Mayor in pocket.His back was against the wall so he accepted Cash's offer. They went to Thompson street and from 49th to 50th they bought every house on the block with cash. This was operation takeover and Cash wasn't playing. He gave the fiends a place to smoke, and live as long as they spent money. Cash had designated smoke houses on the block, and houses that the product was cooked and packaged. He had to get the security set up, cameras in every room, and goons that stood guard at every house heavily armed. It took a few weeks to get every house but in the mean time they asked for the biggest shipment they ever ordered, 100 kilos.

The money started rolling in. A majority of the smokers in the West Philadelphia area made their way to Thompson Street, it was a fiend's sanctuary. If you were spending you had a place to smoke and sleep as long as you woke up spending. This caused friction between other dealers in West until Cash dropped off kilos For 17.5. He was showing love and the city loved him back. For now…

$ $ $ $ $ $ $ $ $ $ $ $ $ $ $ $ $ $

"I want this asshole do you people hear me?" Agent Galvin was in a meeting with his team trying to build a conspiracy case on Cash that would stick, and land him behind bars forever. He needed a good C.I and drugs on the table. He had no solid evidence just some low level punks that gave him some street gossip. That's how he knew about the killing of L and Keith. He checked it out and the report said they killed each other. He pointed to the bulletin board that had two pictures up, Cash and Rome.

Chapter 10

Growing Pains

Over the next couple of months the money was great and the Mayor held up his part of the bargain. Cash had Thompson Street doing 2 million a week and Lansdowne Ave was doing 1.2. It was unbelievable. Cash still was being a daddy and making his relationship with Maria stronger. But as much as they grew closer he and Dallas grew apart. She had to move on with her life, as much as she wanted to be with Cash she couldn't.

Rome still thought about the Feds every day. If he would see a cell soon he was going to enjoy his freedom everyday. He began to be out of town a lot to see the world.They had workers, the operation ran itself. Face made sure every 2 weeks they got there 100 bricks on time faithfully. Rome took trips to Brazil, China, Europe, and different cities in the states like New York where he had a brownstone and a few lady friends.

He was in Harlem with his Spanish girl Jessica. He was suppose to be leaving but Jessica had him going to the store for some condoms because she needed some more dick before her Philly boo left.

"My bad bull!" Rome said as he bumped into a young thug and stepped on his shoe by mistake.

"My bad, what the fuck you mean son? Look at my shits these Bathing Apes bee you got the front all scuffed up!" The Harlem kid barked.

"Yo bull I said mybad, watch ya fuckin mouth."

"What the fuck you say bee?" He came from under his shirt with a long nose .38 pistol. Rome had his 380 in his pocket he was heated a gun was in his face. He could of stayed in Philly for this.

"Yo bull you got it, here take dis. I aint mean to step on them jawns." Rome pulled some money out his pocket and extended his hand to the young thug.The young kid eyes grew when he saw all the money Rome had on him.

"Listen son I need all that! So go back in ya pocket and get the rest." The young New Yorker ordered with the gun at Rome's chest. Rome shook his head, he looked up at the second floor of the building Jessica was in, he was right there. It was early a few people were watching and some just walked by really fast like this was normal.

"Ard bull hold up don't shoot… here." Rome looked around like some one would help him and dug in his pocket.

"Yo son stop fuckin calling me bull!! What the fuck is that?"

POP POP!!! Arrggghhhhh!! The kid yelled in pain.

Rome couldn't go out like that. He squeezed off his 380 when he came out his pocket and hit the kid twice in the leg and hip. He watched the kid fall and ran toward the building. "POP POP POP!!!"

The New Yorker fired three shots from the ground almost hitting Rome as the door closed behind him.

"Jessica A nigga just tried to rob me!! Yo in broad day light with mafuckas walking by. These niggas crazy out here I popped him!" Rome yelled as he came in her apartment. Jessica went to her window and the cops were already outside. Someone pointed up to her window and she stepped back. "Papi the cops outside!" Rome ran over and he saw someone pointing at their window.

"Shit!" Before Rome knew it, the cops were banging on the door. He was being cuffed and they were taking him to the police station.

"That shit was self defense he tried to rob me!" Rome said to the officers who were driving him. "They all say that!"

$ $ $ $ $ $ $ $ $ $ $ $ $ $ $ $ $

Rome had been in the small room cuffed to a table for two hours. No one had come to check on him or even offer a soda. When the door opened he thought he saw a ghost. Special Agent Galvin walked in with a young black guy dressed in urban wear who obviously was an undercover.

"Look what we got here Mr. Rome. Damn attempted murder in front of eye witnesses? You ready to talk now?" Rome looked up at the determined federal agent.

"Lawyer! Lawyer cuz what you got to say I don't wanna hear."

"Meet Agent Donalds. As you can see he is an undercover. I want you to introduce him to Cash and he will build a case from the inside. You do this and I will give you immunity, NO TIME! I need this Rome, so save your ass because when the shit hits the fan in the Feds. It's tag your man or see him on the stand!"

"You must be hard of hearing. Ain't that a law, if I ask for a lawyer all this shit stop? I don't know anybody by the name of Cash. So LAWYER!"

Agent Galvin looked at him and laughed.

"Let's go this ass hole is going to rot in jail. I'm going to make sure of it. Good luck with this gun case in New York!"

Rome stayed on Riker's Island for a week and was bonded out on a $75,000 bond. His lawyer told him the case was weak and the witnesses confirmed Rome story, the most they could do was charge him with the unregistered gun. Since Rome was never arrested before his lawyer said he would be looking at a year and a day under New York guidelines. Rome was free to go and his first stop was to talk to Cash.

Cash was home he had both the kids and was relaxing with Maria. When Rome walked in both the boys screamed Uncle Rome. He hugged them both as he lifted them up. "Whassup nephews I'm back!"

"Whassup bro?" Cash said.

"Tryna beat cases and stack money bull.You know my lawyer talkin a year and a day for that gun. Yo bull how can I leave this shit for that long? We killin em right now!!" He put the kids down and Cash and Rome took the conversation to the den.

"Look chill the fuck out bro. You just keep getting in shit. What happened out there?"

"Some young dickhead tried to rob me. He pulled a gun out on me in broad day light. People was just walking by and watching while he had the jawn to me. I squeezed off on him I wasn't even tryna kill him. I just wanted to back him up so I hit him in the leg and ran." Rome told him about the Feds desperate attempt to flip him and Cash just shook his head. They were really on his ass.

"Look I need some pussy I'm bout to go holla at one of my bitches Rome home bitch. I'm out bull I hit ya jack in a few."

"Welcome home bro!" Cash joked and Rome was out the door.

$ $ $ $ $ $ $ $ $ $ $ $ $ $ $ $ $

Rome was dropping one of his groupies off down 52nd Girard. He looked inside the Donut shop as he waited for the light to change and saw Black Tae posted. He quickly dialed Cash's number because he didn't want to do anything without his ok.

"Yo bull I see dis nigga with the dick problem." At first Cash didn't understand then it clicked. Black Tae had been ducking him good for a long time.

"Where you at Rome?"

"I'm at 52nd Girard."

"I be there in ten minutes. Rome do not lose him!" Cash flew out the door with his gun in hand. He was ready to put Black Tae in his place, and that place was six feet under. He wasn't having anyone disrespect his family and live to tell about it. He was a boss and on this level there was no room for foul play.

Black Tae came out the Donut shop and walked across the street to a small block called Wilton. Rome watched from the vacant lot next to the Chinese store. He couldn't let him get away so he walked across the street as Black Tae took a piss in the alley. Black Tae was shaking his dick when he felt the steel in his back.

"Ya dick always get you in trouble bull." Black Tae was caught off guard he didn't know who it was he couldn't see the face. Rome was up close he couldn't move.

"Don't move nigga or I will save a lot of time. Chill!"

"What I do bull? You got the wrong nigga!" Rome phone vibrated and Rome told him pull up on Wilton by the alley fast. Cash pulled up with the Mac on his lap. "Let's go!"

Rome gripped Tae up by his collar and put him in the backseat.

"YOOO what the fuck y'all doing wit Tae. YOOOO!" Someone yelled out spotting Rome muscle Black Tae.

"BDDDDDDDDDDDDDDDDAAATTTTTTT BDDDDDDDDAAATTTTT!!!!" Cash let off the Mac 10 and a wave of bullets ripped through the kid with with the big mouth. Black Tae used that time to sucker punch Rome and daze him in the back seat. He jumped out and Cash looked back to see Rome lip leaking.

"You good nigga wake up!!" Cash hopped out and let another lead shower pour up the block as Black Tae ran. Cash caught em in the back and calf crippling him to the concrete.

"Got you!" He ran up on him as he crawled leaving a blood trail on the side walk. "Turn around!" Black Tae refused to face him.

"Fuck you nigga!!!" He yelled on his stomach. Cash placed the Mac to the back of his head. "Do it nigga! All this over a bitch. I aint even fuck her!" Black Tae said still with his face down on the ground.

"It's the principal, niggas need to watch who they disrespect!" He pulled the trigger letting the bullets crack his scull and splattered his brains.

"Let's go let's go!!"Rome screamed as he backed up the car for Cash to get in.

$ $ $ $ $ $ $ $ $ $ $ $ $ $ $ $ $

Maria put her son to sleep and got in the shower. The water dripped off her body and her mind drifted slowly as the heat eased her. She had thoughts of Cash getting shot and seeing him in a casket. Police sirens rang in her ears as if she was right there. The images were so vivid she was at a grave yard and someone was putting flowers on a grave. It was Cash he was still alive, she ran to him and fell when she went through his body. She fell face first onto the dirt and looked up at the name on the tombstone.

"Baby baby baby....baby baby snap out of it!!" Cash said slapping Maria's naked butt.

"Oouuchh nigga!" she turned the water off.

"What the fuck was you thinking about or you high?"

"Nothing why you come in all hype what's wrong?" Cash was her heart she knew when something was wrong with him. He sweats and breaths hard. She knew his symptoms like she was his personal Doctor.

"I murdered dat nigga baby! I did that shit for you, he dead!"

"Who, why Cash What happened?"

"That nigga that pulled his dick out on you. I caught him. Niggas not fucking wit mine period. You my family so fuck him that's for you!"

Maria shook her head she told him to leave that situation alone, Black Tae peoples all was from the street. Cash saw she was looking confused so he pulled her close.

"Whats wrong babe?"

"Bull peoples in that life baby. You think they gonna let that ride? Be careful now I know they crazy!"

"I hear you babe but me and mine will take care of that. You just get dat ass on that bed I wanna taste ya butt since you fresh out the shower." Cash slapped her booty and it jiggled.

"You nasty boy!"

$ $ $ $ $ $ $ $ $ $ $ $ $ $ $ $ $

Over on 52nd street the block was going crazy. Black Tae's people wanted to know what was up and who was responsible. Lips were locked and if their reputation didn't make believers out of people, seeing it live in color really helped make their mind up. Mind your business Cash and Rome are not to be fucked with!!!

"You dead nigga! Bow bow." The kid said who played with his friend they both were no older then 6.

"Ard let me be Cash and you be Black!" The other kid said.

"Noooo im Cash dickhead!"

Headz was still in tears on the block Tae was his cousin and he wasn't having it. He heard the kids playing and walked over.

"What the fuck y'all playing youngbulls?" The kids looked up at Headz who was short and darkskin. His eyes were low and red.

"We playin Cash and Rome but we had to be Black for the shooting scene because it's only two of us. I told him I wanted to be Cash he a gangster for real." The kid spoke as if the death inspired him. They were misguided youth coming up in a concrete jungle full of snakes, rats, and wolves.

"That bitch ass nigga aint no gangster!! You need to be a doctor fuck being a gangster. Get y'all lil bad ass in the house, where ya momma at?"

"Fuck outta here oldhead!" The other kid said. Headz couldn't believe his ears but he got the information he needed without paying or shooting anybody. He walked down the street to get his brother Leek Mobb. It was time to let a few people join his cousin and Cash and Rome were top on the list.

"Yo bro don't you know where Cash bitch get her hair done at?" Headz asked his older brother Leek Mobb who was just as hurt as he was of the death of Black Tae.

"Yeah my girl and his girl go to the same shop why whassup?"

"I want to make him feel how I'm feeling. Get dat bitch!" Leek Mobb wasn't with that but this was his family and revenge was due.

"Whoa Headz you tryna get his bitch you drawin lets just air that nigga and his boy!"

"Stop bitchin nigga I got this is you ridin or what cuz we getting paid too!?"

"Fuck it just let me know the plan."

For the next couple weeks Leek Mobb watched Maria from the hair dresser. She came every Friday and he was right there parked outside every time. Leek Mobb followed her home. He knew where she lived and where her kid went to school.After only a few weeks he had her schedule down to a science. Leek Mobb sat outside of Cash's house and watched him get in his car and pull off with the kids. He made the phone call.

"Yeah he gone what you want me to do?"

$ $ $ $ $ $ $ $ $ $ $ $ $ $ $ $ $

"Daddy when we all going to live together? His son asked from the back seat.

"I don't know but even if we don't live together we still love each other no matter what. You know that right? You know ya daddy love both y'all to death right?"

"I know that daddy I just want to be with my brother every day!" Cash loved how smart his kids were they really made him happy. He thought of his father at that moment and remembered how much he missed. His dad died in a car accident speeding trying to get to his 5 grade graduation. All his memories of him were when he was a child. He always wanted to make him proud. Cash's phone vibrated taking him from his thoughts. The number was blocked but he still answered.

"Yo who dis?"

"Damn ya baby mom look good what that pussy hittin for bull?"

"What who the fuck is this?"

"This the nigga that got ya bitch. Now listen the fuck up before I slap dis bitch wit my dick and bruise her cheek. Get me $250,000 in an hour have my shit ready I hit you back." Cash heart began to speed up and he looked back at his kids. He pulled over on the side of the road to talk.

"Motherfucka is you crazy you really wanna die. I will put you in a fuckin bag boy let me talk to her right now or you aint getting shit!" He whispered trying to be calm without disturbing his boys as they fight over the toy train.

"Calm down gangster here she go. CAAAASSSSHHH!"

"Nigga let my girl go you coward. See me in the street nigga! Let her go!"

"One hour! And gangster, $500,000 now since you playing Sosa." The line went dead. It didn't matter what amount they said, Cash had it, and was giving his last to save his girl. For $500,000 he would have her back A.s.a.p! Cash made a U turn and hurried back home.It wasn't a dream his nightmare became reality. Maria was gone and the front door was off the hinges. "Fuccccck!" He called Rome and told him meet him at Maria's house and bring Dallas to watch the boys.

When Rome got there Cash had put the boys to sleep and was waiting downstairs with stacks of money all over the living room. He went in his safe and collected the 500 easy. He would make it back in a week. His main concern was getting Maria back safe. He knew this was a part of the game, he just prayed he never saw it, like death and jail. Dallas and Rome saw all that money and the look on Cash's face and knew something was terribly wrong.

"Yo bull what the fuck is going on?"

“They got her bull…they got Maria…they want 500 racks or you already know!”

“Who? When the fuck this happen?” Dallas burst out crying Maria was her best friend and like a sister. Now she was kidnapped by some goons.

“I don’t fuckin know who! They called me when I left her crib so they had to be watching me. Ayo I need my baby back shit will get real ugly if I don’t get my shorty back home with my son! He can’t lose his mom bro. I got the money, please God don’t let these cowards harm my baby!” Cash’s heart was broken, he knew this was all his fault. The life he chose had caught up to him so many times before but this was the one that hurt the most. The clock was ticking and Cash’s phone rang exactly an hour later from a blocked number. “Hello.”

“You got my money?”

“Yeah yeah I got the money just don’t hurt my girl yo I swear to God I got all your money just don’t involve my family!”

“Nigga fuck ya family you aint give a fuck about mine! Drop that money off at the payphone on 52nd Girard. Drop it off and leave! I will call after I count the money to tell you where to pick this sexy ass bitch up. Don’t try no funny shit bull or before I blow dis bitch head off, I will be the last to fuck her!” CLICK

Cash went to drop the money off on 52nd. He looked around hoping it wasn’t an ambush with the heavy duffel bag over his shoulder. He placed it on the ground by the pay phone and his phone vibrated.

"Keep walking don't look behind you, I will call you in a few after I count it." Cash did as instructed and walked all the way to his car without looking back. "Now drive off I don't want to see you in this area." Cash followed the demands and left praying for that next phone call.

Leek Mobb scooped the duffel bag up as Cash pulled off. He hopped in his car and took out a few stacks and began to tuck them in his glove box and arm rest. He drove to the spot Headz held Maria hostage at. He walked in with the bag over his shoulder.

"I got the money bro!" Headz seen the husky bag and his mind raced on what he would buy first. He had never had so much money at once and he had so many plans. It was his time to ball! He felt he deserved it for all his pain and suffering. He opened the bag up and smelled the money. "Hmmmmmm that shit smell so good!" Headz pulled his gun from his waist and walked to the back room where Maria was held captive blindfolded and tied to a chair.

"Baby girl ya man paid that tab!" Maria body jerked as she heard the voice of the freak that kept rubbing his dick on her lips and making her suck it slow.

"So you letting me go right? I can go home now you got the money just let me go. Pleaaaassse just let me go I don't know you!" Headz walked up to her and placed the gun to her head. One shot plastered her brains on the wall.

"It never was about the money shorty!" Leek Mobb came in after the shot and saw the girl leaned over in the chair with half her head blown off. It was messy.

"Damn bro did you have to kill her tho?"

"Stop bitchin fuck dis bitch! Here!" Headz gave him some stacks from the money , it was only 50 grand. Leek Mobb just shook his head. They were in this together and his own brother was crossing him.

"Where the rest of my chicken at bull?"

"You aint kill shit bro! You scooped dat bitch up, for that I give you 50!" Headz laughed and his brother just lowered his head. That's why he had tucked those stacks because he knew Headz would try to jerk him. Headz dialed Cash's number. "Hello?"

"You miss this bitch?"

"Yo bull let me speak to her I gave you the money now let me get my shorty back!!"

"If you can bring hoes back from the dead you a bad mafucka. That's for my peoples nigga!!" The line went dead.

"NOOOOOOOOOOOOOOOOOOOOOO!!!!!" If this wasn't the slap in the face to get him out the game he didn't know what would do it. He cried out in heartache knowing his lover and wifey was gone. Cash had lost his soul and the game had no love for her. His moves caused the death of his heart and the streets did it. He would avenge her death if that was last thing he did. She was not being taken away from his family without someone feeling the same pain times 10. He was about to paint the city red and it was about to begin with Black Tae's family, he just didn't know who first. It was going down and there was nowhere they could hide. Money talks and with 100 grand on your head in the street, your own momma will unlock the door for your shooter, where he was from.

Chapter 11

Headaches

The next few days Cash isolated his self in his condo. He left the kids with Dallas and blocked the world out. He knew his woman was gone because of him and he hated his self for it and wished he could turn back the hands of time. This game had brought so much money in his life he was blind at what it also took away from it. He couldn't sit in that Church for the funeral. He was too emotional so he left. The whole West Philly came out to support Maria with t-shirts with her face. Others came just to have said they were there, but mostly on the strength of it being Cash's girl. The Feds were in the cut taking pictures building their case and seeing who was who. Cash just got a bottle of Hennessy and drowned in the brown.

While Cash was morning, Rome was in the streets trying to get results. Maria was like his little sister and he felt just as much heartache as Cash. He couldn't believe how foul guys got in this game. It was kill or be killed, shoot or get shot.

"Hello is this Rome I got some info on what you been looking for?"

"Who the fuck is this?" The female voice didn't sound familiar. She told him to come to her house and they could talk there. Rome asked the address and made his way to North Philly. When he got outside the apartment building he called the girl back. She told him to come to apt 305. Rome put his 40 in his waist and got out. He knocked two times and the door opened. The girl was on the big side and looked sloppy. Rome walked in her small apartment and saw two roaches climbing the wall, it was like they stopped to say hello and kept moving.

"What you got me up here for this shit better be good?"

"You giving a 100 grand to get you the niggas that did that shit to Cash girl right?"

"Talk shorty do you know something because I could be in these streets finding it out myself?"

"My ex boyfriend came by earliar with a lot of money and he always broke so I knew he just robbed somebody. He told me his brother killed Maria and got all this money from her dude. He be back in a few." Rome couldn't believe his ears, they found them.

"Who ya dude and who is his brother?"

"My ex name Leek Mobb and his brother some short hot head name Headz."

Rome pulled out his gun and slapped her in the face with it.

"Let's wait for ya ex then!" She fell to the floor from the hard blow.

Two hours later Rome watched as the doorknob turned to the apartment and Leek Mobb walked in. The first thing he saw was his baby bleeding from the head on the floor. Then he was joining her side as Rome cracked him in the head with the gun as well knocking him out cold. He hit up Cash and told him where he was and to get there like yesterday.

$ $ $ $ $ $ $ $ $ $ $ $ $ $ $ $ $

When Cash got the call from Rome he got up so fast you would of thought he was on fire. He flew out the house and hopped in his car. Cash knew the Feds might be watching so he made a few turns, then a U turn. When he thought he was clear he made a few more turns to see if he was being tailed. No one was behind him for a while so he mashed the gas to get to North Philly.

Cash knocked on the door of the apartment and Rome let him in. He saw Leek Mobb and some fat chick tied up on the couch bleeding. He pulled out his gun and pressed it against Leek Mobb's scull as he begged him not to shoot. He claimed it wasn't him it was his brother.

"Wait bro not yet!"

"Listen I got a plan for this clown," Rome interjected before Cash blew his head off.

"We gotta think about Maria!!" Cash mushed the gun in Leek Mobbs face. "My baby gone she would want this motherfucker dead. You hear me, dead nigga!" Cash yelled and tears streamed down his face. He was enraged and vengeance was the only medicine that would ease his pain.

"Where ya brother stay at nigga?"

"He don't live there no more he about to leave the city soon. He hotel hopping, just fucking bitches and spending money. I swear to God if I knew where he was I would tell you!" Leek Mobb screamed out trying to save his own life. Rome pulled Cash back and whispered in his ear.

"Chill bro I got a plan so just relax. We going to let him live for now!"

"What are you doing Rome?" Cash asked with confusion.

"He had something to do with it too! This nigga was in on it!"

“Trust me my nigga we going to let him live for now. Yo bull you good stop bitchin we aint gonna pop you.” Rome said tapping his head with the gun as he looked him in the eyes.

“ BOC BOC BOC!!!”

“NOOOOOOOOOOOOOOOOOOOOOOOOOOOOO!!! Leek mob screamed out as Cash fired three shots into his big girl’s chest. She fell over onto her stomach and blood poured from the huge holes in her flesh. They left Leek Mobb still breathing and tied up next to his big bitch.

“Why we aint off that nigga bro? What you got on ya mind?” Cash said when they got back to his spot. Rome started to break down his master plan.

“Listen bro! I found Gina nasty ass, the bitch that gave Bonez that shit! I seen her a few weeks ago lookin like trash. I put her in this program to clean her up and she came back like cooked crack. She ready to do whatever for me, she say I helped her get her life back on track. I figure we put her on Leek Mobb and let that situation handle it self. Then when she done her job, let Bonez off her!”

“I like that, I like that! When we find Headz tho it’s off with his head. No fuckin excuses he done and I hope he don’t think he can hide. Money talks and somebody gonna let us know something.”

$ $ $ $ $ $ $ $ $ $ $ $ $ $ $ $ $

Headz was having the time of his life. He didn't realize having money made you so happy. He had purchased a 2005 S600 Benz, some ice to flood his neck and wrist, and was in the strip clubs tricking every night. He told his self he would leave in another week. Headz just wanted to fuck every bitch he could before he left and never looked back at this city again.

"I'm tryna tell you shorty this life I live so real, niggas hate me. I'm out here riding around and getting it. Look at me?" Headz told his thick stripper friend who was passenger seat. He had walked in flashing all this money so she went over grabbed his dick and told him a price he couldn't turn down for the pussy. She knew all the ballers that came to her club and he was new.

They got to his hotel room and Headz laid on the king size bed. He was the size of Kevin Hart so he looked so small in the middle of the bed she almost laughed.

"Get them clothes off shorty I wanna see ass and titties all night!" He went in his pocket and threw some money in the air.

"Okay baller let me see something." She stripped down to her birthday suit and climbed on the bed and onto his face.

"Eat that pussy baby!!! Awwwww shit mommy love it!" She said as she gyrated on his tongue and Headz swallowed her juices. She came twice and got up to go to the bathroom.

"Damn that pussy taste good! No wonder they call you Juicy!" Headz said wiping his face dry of her wetness. He heard the shower run and began to roll up a Dutch.

When the Dutch was almost over he noticed his thick goddess hadn't emerged from the bathroom yet. Headz got up high from the exotic weed he was still smoking. He walked toward the bathroom.

"Damn girl I know you got a lot of ass to wash but damn!" He knocked on the door and it slowly opened. "Bout time c'mon!" The steam from the shower had the bathroom cloudy and hot. The water was still running. It opened all the way and Cash greeted him with a blow to the mouth with his gun knocking out both his front teeth. "Arrrrggghhhhhhh!" Headz fell back onto the floor holding his mouth. He looked on the dresser and saw his gun so far away. Cash went across his face even harder. Juicy came from the bathroom fully clothed. "Good looking girl let Rome in." She walked over to the door and Rome walked in.

"Whassup baller?" Headz was set up, he had fallen for the big butt and a smile. Juicy winked at him and left. He shook his head he knew he was dead. He looked up at Cash who had the gun in his face.

"Ayo the rest of the money in the trunk of the Benz. I swear that's all I got left I didn't do it! It was my brother he made me please get the gun out my face."

"You killed my girl nigga! My baby's mother!! You got these chains on and that fuckin watch on cuz of my money! Nigga gimmie that shit!" Headz quickly removed his two diamond chains and his big face gold Rolex. He tossed them on the bed and scooted closer to the wall as Rome and Cash stood over him with weapons.

"Yo bull you killed my cousin what was I suppose to do. Let that shit ride? FUCK DAT!" Cash told Rome to get his keys and drive the Benz somewhere and torch it, he would finish this.

"What nigga? Naw we leave together, do him and let's go Cash, c'mon!!" Cash just nodded his head no. He pulled some plastic gloves from his pocket and put them on.

"My nigga… just go I got this! Its going to be ugly." Rome did as he was told and left. "Mariaaaaa baby I got him! I got him baby!" Gimmie ya i.d bitch!" Headz passed him his wallet and Cash went through it. He looked at a picture of Headz with a female and two little boys.

"This ya family bro? You just leaving them huh?" Cash picked up Headz gun from the table and the worst pistol whipping none to man began. Cash beat his face in until he stopped breathing, it was a bloody massacre.

$ $ $ $ $ $ $ $ $ $ $ $ $ $ $ $ $

"Can I help you?" The woman asked with a confused look on her face as she saw Cash standing at her door at 10:30 at night. He lifted the gun and pointed it at her head. He looked her in her eyes with a cold stare and spoke.

"Who all in the house with you?" She tried to turn and run but Cash was on her heels. He grabbed her by the back of her neck and back handed her. She flew to the floor screaming. "Shut the fuck up!" He put the gun in her mouth and she let her cries subside. He removed the gun and she blurted out. "It aint no money in the house!! I swear he took all of it!" Cash didn't want to do this but this was a message for the streets. He had no heart so there was no remorse or sympathy. They didn't have any for

Maria. Then flashes of her smile, her naked body, her long hair, it was so vivid. A tear came down his face and he pressed the gun to her head.

"She gone! She not coming back! Tell her I love her when you get there." BOOM!!! He fired his gun letting the single bullet end her life. Cries from a baby burst out upstairs, and Cash went to see. He saw the two boys in their separate beds in their room. They were only 2 and 3 and both crying loudly.

"He took my heart this y'all daddy fault!" Then he raised the gun.

Chapter 12

Summer Time

The first week of summer had the streets buzzing. The ladies were in the shortest skirts, the swimming pools were popping, and the water plugs were spraying kids and cars that came by. The cooks outs and block parties were jamming loud music and the sun gave everyone a bright day!

Cash had been drinking a lot lately, popping pills and still heavy on the Haze. It helped him cope with the death of his girl 4 months ago that he still blamed his self for. He just couldn't stop now, his hunger for money and power fueled his desire to hold his position down. He and Dallas had been getting closer since Maria passing. They moved outside the city with boths his kids. After Leek Mobb had found out where he lived he didn't feel safe resting his head in the city anymore. He didn't even allow Dallas to go to Philly. She went to medical school and was a mom. He loved the fact both his kids were both under the same room. Both his boys were hurt by Maria's death but they built a bond as brothers that was incredible.

Rome still was waiting on his court date to get his time. His lawyer was giving him as much time on the street before his day as he could. He was happy all he had to do was a year and a day. He just didn't want to leave his right hand man at a time like this, when he needed him to be there.

"Where you going all sexy?" Dallas asked Cash who was fully dressed with his West Philly chain dangling from his neck sparkling. His waves were on swim and his shape up was Steve Harvey sharp. Cash had a lime green Polo t-shirt with the dark blue horse on it, some dark blue Polo cargo shorts and some fresh construction Timberlands.

"We out get ya ass up. We going shoppin!" Cash went to wait in the Range Rover.

After almost listening to the whole Black Album, Dallas and the kids finally came from the house. He looked at Dallas as she walked in those tight jeans and red bottoms, her belly shirt exposed her flat stomach. This was his girl now and he was so happy, but felt bad at the same time. Every time they had sex or kissed he just thought of Maria, and the guilt set in. He loved her and she stood by his side and never left no matter how much he pushed her away or cursed her out.

"What you lookin at?" Dallas said as she put the kids in their booster seats in the back of the truck.

"That lil fat ass that jawn pokin out today!" Cash joked and they were off to the mall. They walked through K.O.P as a family and Cash went straight to the Foot Locker. When he and Dallas came in with the boys all eyes were on them. He saw Wydia with her referee Foot Locker shirt on walking toward him. They had'nt seen each other since he had to knock her boyfriend out. He remembered how good her dick suck was and smiled.

"Heeeeyyy Cash I see you have ya cute little boys with you," Wydia said ignoring Dallas who was right there with them.

"Yeah and his girl and you are?" Dallas said with attitude.

"Wydia we go back nothing major. So what you need Cash I can get you a discount?"

Cash shook his head and walked over to the Jordan foot wear for kids.

"Let me get all three of the newest J's Two a piece in a 6 and a 7." Wydia checked the bottom of the shoes to see if they had those sizes and they did. "Okay we got them. Anything else…you like and want!" Dallas didn't hear her but Cash knew what she was referring to.

"Just get me two pair of buttas and some white Shells in a10." She got his stuff together and he paid in cash. Wydia wrote her new number down on the receipt hoping he would call.

As they came out the Gucci store Dallas just looked at him. He was the love of her life. She never felt this way about another person before.

"Why you spend all that money in there babe?" Cash had dropped 10 racks in the Gucci store like it was a $100 dollars. He looked down at all his bags and smiled.

"Cash you never let the money change you, you always been low key. That's what attracted me to you. You had it but didn't flaunt it. What seperates you from so many niggas that get money is you think of the risk of this shit. You have goals like the club. Niggas wanna trap forever!" Cash agree with her and realized he wasn't like the rest of the drug dealers his age. When they were copping big cars and splurging. He was trying to flip the next dollar and stack the one after that.

"Look you only live once and I'm about to start enjoying my chicken! If I get popped tomorrow and check out what did I do? Nothing, I got a Range I barely drive and its old now, and this ice! I get money and don't really stunt! Shit bout to change a lil bit"

They dropped the boys off at Dallas aunt's house and headed home. Cash was going in the basement and called up to Dallas.

"Ayo get that book bag in the living room and dump that money out on the bed. As she did that, Cash went to get his stash of pills he had in the basement. He popped two blues and washed it down with Hennessy and cleared his throat. "Ahhhhh needed that!" He walked in on Dallas who had all the stacks of money all over the bed.

"Why you needed me to dump it all out?"

"Just take ya clothes off babe!"

"For what?"

"Just do it D." Cash had a lustful look in eyes and Dallas knew it was Mr. Nasty time.

Dallas took every piece of clothing off and Cash hit the stereo. Keyshia Cole's Love came through the speakers. He stripped down to his socks and left his chain on. He spread her legs and tasted her sweet juices. Dallas arched her back and clutched hundred dollar bills as the tingling sensation from her clit shot up her back. She hit Cash with a stack of money on the top of his head, she cuffed her breast and bit her bottom lip.

"Ooh God!" She purred and grinded her pussy against his wet tongue swiftly.

Cash looked up at her while she was in pure pleasure. "You taste soooo good baby!" He went back in face first and continued his tongue attack on the pussy.

"Awwwww baby eat dat pussy…right there right there!" Dallas came and Cash stood up stiff as a dead body.

"Turn around!" He demanded and she obeyed as her dripping pussy awaited his stiffness. He picked up a stack of money and started making it rain on her before he slid in and pounded away. After a long hour of different positions Cash rolled over with a body full of sweat. The loose bills stuck to his naked body.

"Ewwww!" Dallas peeled a wet Benjamin from his back.

"You acting like you won't still spend it!"

"Whatever boy! What did you take cuz you would not stop baby? You was all up in me!"

"Nothing I just love ya pussy babe!" He kissed her lips and stood up.

"Where you going now?"

"I got to handle some business with Rome. You good?"

"Hell yeah I'm good you fucked the shit outta me. You just gonna leave me after the best sex we ever had?"

"I got to handle some shit. Do me a favor and count this money let me know how much it is."

"Whatever Cash that's what you wanted me to do in the first place!"

"I'm out!" Cash got dressed and went to meet up with Rome.

$ $ $ $ $ $ $ $ $ $ $ $ $ $ $ $ $

Rome and Cash pulled up at the Cadillac dealership and Rome was ready to stunt just as much as Cash.

"You sure about this bro? You so low key and shit! No you tryna up and ball?" Rome asked as they sat in the car.

"I'm ready to show niggas who really getting money out here. What's the use of having all this fuckin chicken if you can't spend it? Let's go be young bosses in this jawn!" Cash grabbed the Gucci duffel on the back seat and they walked into the Cadillac Dealership ready to ball out! It was time to shine.

They walked around the lot for a while and Cash was ready. He saw a few vehicles that caught his attention but the black CTS had him stuck. He flagged a salesman over and he quickly came to his aid. "Hello sir can I help you?"

"Yeah I want this pretty bitch right here and the new Escalade in black!"

"Sir do you realize how much that is?" Cash unzipped the Gucci bag exposing the stacks of money inside. The salesman eyes grew wide and he told Cash to follow him. Money talks!

Rome had his mind made up and he was getting the Escalade truck with the butterfly doors, all white everything. Rome saw Cash signing some paperwork in the office and slid in with him.

"I need one too bull.You hookin us up?" Rome asked the salesman.

He told Rome they would have to order the part for his doors so it would be a few days before he could come get his truck. Cash paid $110,000 cash money and the man passed off the keys. Rome paid $62,000 and they went to check out the new rides.

"You drive the truck I'm a whip the CTS." He handed Rome the keys.

"What about the car we drove up here." Rome asked referring to Cash's squader.

"Leave that bullshit you don't see what we driving. Fuck that bucket!"

The duo drove through the streets of West Philly like young Kings. It wasn't a lot of people in the city making moves like they were illegally. West Philly was Cash, and if you sold coke you got it from him, and if you smoked it from 2002 to 2005 it was an 87% chance it came from his supply. Face had Cash moving 500 kilos a month and wasn't nothing touching his quality in the city at that time. Cash wasn't dumb at all. He began passing off money to all the o.gs of the game in his area as a sense of paying homage. He knew people came before him and there would be people after. He donated to local public schools and rec centers. He still remembered the look on his principals's face when he dropped off $75,000 for the school. He just wanted to make sure for the time being his spot was secure. The love he received from the community in return was undeniable. Everyone knew his name, he was like a ghetto Robin Hood.

When they pulled up at Cash's home Dallas was in the garage cleaning up. She saw two tinted luxury vehicles pull up in her driveway.

"I see y'all doing it big. Hey Rome!!" Dallas said as they both got out the cars.

"Whassup D let me find out you cleaning up?" Rome said.

"What boy I clean! Who else gonna do it, his big head ass not? I like these and this truck sexy ass shit." Dallas ran her finger across the hood.

"You like that baby?" Cash asked with a smile.

"Hell yeah this the new jawn?"

"Yeah all for my baby! That's you!" Dallas jumped up and into his arms. He caught her and she planted kisses all over his face.

"Thank you, thank you, I love you thank you!" She got down and got in her new truck and beeped the horn.

"Babe I'm out I be back later. How much money was in the bag?"

"It was 285!"

"Happy birthday that's you!" Dallas birthday was this weekend she would be 23 and with two early gifts as good as these, she had nothing to look forward to. What she did know was Cash loved her. She gave her man a wet kiss and let him go about his business.

Chapter 13

Reality Check

"Hello Mr. Davis." Rome was still half sleep but he knew that voice, it was his lawyer. He sat up in bed to listen and smiled at the two ladies still sleep in his bed. He popped an x pill and was going hard all night.

"Yo whassup whats the verdict?"

"They don't want any more continued court dates."

"So what you saying bull?"

"The prosecutor and the judge on my ass. It's been a year since your case. I have everything set up, you turn yourself in Friday and start this sentence and be home next year." Rome thought about the time he was facing. He had put this day in the back of his head. Now it was time to face the music and go do this time like a G. A year and a day wasn't forever, and it wasn't a dirt nap either. His last days he just fucked ,smoked and fucked some more. Cash drove him to the jail and they smoke haze the whole ride there talking about the good times.

"Damn bro I guess this it until next year. Make sure you ball for me and please fuck every light skin bitch with a fat ass just for me!" They laughed and talked about the times before the money and street fame.

"Keep ya head up bull. This time or no time can hold a real nigga down!

I'll be out here when you done so remember you good!" Rome shook his best friend's hand for the last time for a while.

"Get at me!" Then Rome stepped out the car to self surrender. As Cash watched his brother from another leave him to go start his bid reality set in. Cash didn't want to see a cell. He didn't want to be stripped of his rights and treated like an animal. He was grown and had been taking care of his self since he was 11, he couldn't be told when to eat sleep and shit. His club was almost done the contractors had everything they needed and soon he would be at the grand opening to Club Faith. When his club was finished and Rome was home he made his mind up to step away from the drug game. People weren't playing fair and times have changed. The loyalty and respect is gone. The streets will turn your heart cold and Cash wanted his to melt back to normal.

$ $ $ $ $ $ $ $ $ $ $ $ $ $ $ $ $

"Maria…Maria….Baby I knew you would come back to me. Maria…Maria where you going? Nooooooooo baby don't leave me! Noooooooooooo!!!" Cash woke up in a cold sweat shivering. Dallas was use to these nightmares by now. Cash would have the same nightmare of Maria coming back to him and then she would look at him and run. He would chase her for what seemed like miles in his dream. Then when he caught up with her she had her head blown off.

"Baby it's just a nightmare. It's okay c'mere." She pulled him closer like a small child and rocked him in her arms. His phone rang and he looked at the time it was 3am.

"Yo who dis?"

"It's Gina I did it."

"Bitch don't call my phone this late I'm with my family sleeping! What the fuck is wrong with you?"

"You told me to call you since Rome was locked up when I did it. I fucked Leek last night."

"I be at ya spot at 3 tomorrow. Make sure you home!!"

"Alright. Please Cash don't do anything to Leek I think I." CLICK

Cash hung up on her before she could finish. Gina had slowly fallen in love by mistake, she couldn't help herself. Leek was her type, and the time they spent together she really could be herself and communicate and he actually listened.

"Who was that?" Dallas snapped.

"That trick Gina."

"Ok what the fuck she callin you for?" Dallas knew she was a whore and had that package and was giving it to any nigga who was ignorant enough to fuck her without a condom.

"I gave her a job."

"Please Cash don't do nothing with that girl or do nothing to her. You need to leave all this shit alone you gonna risk everything."

"Dallas this bitch gave my blood H.I.V. My cousin! I'm a handle that!"

She knew what that meant and she wasn't about to argue. Cash had emotionally and mentally changed. He became cold and heartless she just wished he got out before he become dead. Cash woke the next day at 2:30 and quickly dialed Gina.

"Ayo you home?"

“Yeah I’m home Cash what’s wrong you sound upset?”

“Nothing I just don’t like being late. Don’t go no where, I’m comin!

Cash got in his CTS and went to pick up Bonez and they went toward Gina’s house. Bonez was still in the blind about where Cash was taking him.

“What’s good Cash? Where we going?”

“I got a surprise for you, so just fall back.”

They pulled up in front of Gina’s house and they walked in, when Bonez saw Gina he snapped.

“Bitch you gave me the ninja,” Bonez smacked Gina, she hit the floor hard. “Why you do that to me, I’ll kill you hoe!!!” *Smack, Smack, Smack.*

Hard vicious backhands and open palm smacks to her face swelled her up immediately. Bonez beat Gina to the kitchen, than back to the living room. Cash pulled out his 380 and gave it to Bone.

“Do that bitch,” Cash said.

“Please don’t kill me, please don’t kill me. I want to live, please!” Gina begged for her life. She had found love, a new way of thinking, and a path towards happiness. She wanted to live now more than ever, she saw her life flash before her eyes and prayed for Leek Mobb. She wanted one last kiss.

Bonez put the gun to her head and tears came down his face.

“I can’t do it Cash! I can’t kill her cuz!”

"What nigga? This bitch killed you! She gave you that shit! You gonna die from that shit, shoot dat bitch!" Bonez dropped the gun to the floor.This wasn't his style. It wasn't in his heart to kill her, not a female. They both were just as wrong and she didn't know she had it.

"I'm not you Cash, I'm not a killer! This a female cuz! As much as I wanna blow her head off for this shit I can't."

"Nigga this aint no female, this a bitch! A dirty one!" Cash picked up the gun and hit Gina across the face with it. Her cheek split and blood gushed from her face as she fell to her knees. Her head bobbed back and forth she was about to pass out.

"I aint got no picks!!!" BOOM,BOOM!"

Cash put a hole in Gina's head and chest. He had no remorse he lived by morals, and you don't pass HIV and live to do it again! Cash was not letting that ride so if his cousin couldn't do it, he would!

"Fuck that bitch cuz! It aint no cure for that! Fuck dat bitch!"

"I know but I couldn't do it." Bonez shook his head. He remembered days of vicious thoughts he had to place harm to Gina. He hated her so much for giving him this disease he couldn't wait for the day he ran into her again. Now she was here and he had the chance, but his heart wouldn't allow him to.

"Well I did. All you can do is live cuz. Take your medicine and chase that rap dream. You nice bite these rappers heads off." Cash hugged his cousin and they left Gina in a pool of blood. Bonez was ready to put this behind him and move on with his life. Bonez closed the door and looked back one last time before he hopped in the car with Cash.

"Rest in peace shorty."

Chapter 14

Now Or Never

It had been 8 months since Rome had been locked up. Cash was handling everything on a street really building his street presence now that his top goon was locked up. Now he had to come from behind the scenes and handle business. He had to hit the hood and check the work. When the shipment came in got the muscle and moved it to where it got cooked and bagged. He had to collect the large amounts of money. If someone wanted more then 5 you saw him.

Cash had got a call one of the spots on Thompson street was coming up short. So he had to check that out because that meant someone was stealing. Cash parked up and headed in the spot that was coming up short. His man Flamez ran this spot and he knew he wasn't stealing they were close and he fed him well. Cash checked the security monitor and it was off.

"Ayo Flamez whassup with this screen that's blacked out?"

"That shit been messed up for about a week bro!"

"How long my bread been coming up short?"

"About a week."

"And this monitor for the spot coming up short?"

"Yeah why?"

"Are you dumb motherfucker c'mon!!"

"Where we going?"

"Lets go!!!!!!!!!!!!!!!!!" Cash barked ready to snap. Cash went to the room that was giving up shorts in the spot to check the camera that was in that room. This was one of the cash rooms, it didn't surprise Cash. Someone got tempted and would be made example of. Everyone in the cash rooms were naked, and security was in the room with them unarmed. They got paid to just watch the counters.They watched the counters and the door man checks them when they go in and out, and the cameras watch them all. Cash had a million dollar operation so he had to be cautious. Being that Cash never showed up everyone in the room paused they knew something was up. "People we got sticky fingers in this jawn? C'mon we family in here! I'm giving you 5 grand a week to count money. You don't get no fuckin tips. Go get a job and see what you get! Please I hate when people bite the hand that feed them. I really don't like that!" Everyone was quiet as Cash walked over to the camera that was suppose to be broken. He chuckled and saw it wasn't even plugged up. He plugged it in and looked at Flamez with a vicious glare. Either he was dumb as hell or had something to do with it. That was his homie he didn't want to think he was a snake so he gave him a pass as just being dumb as hell.

"Look Flamez the problem right here. Shit wasn't even plugged up. This ya trap crib you suppose to be on point. Do I need someone else to take ya place. You don't like what I pay you so you wanna steal from me?"

"Cash this me nigga I aint steal shit!"

"Well you dumb as hell and this aint going to be for you! I can't hire you and lose money! So if you aint stealing, somebody is! So who stealing my shit?" Cash pulled his gun and walked around the room.

"I don't know bro!"

"Listen I'm going to make this easy for one or two or all of you who have something to do with it. Speak up if you been stealing. Do it! I got 50 racks for you just for being real. I'm not going to lie your fired but you got 50 racks!" The room was quiet and eyes looked at other eyes to see who would step up. Who would reveal themselves?

"Ayo Cash I tucked a few thousand!" One of his workers stepped up who was just a watcher of the counters.

"See this is a man. He kept it real I respect this man. He a dead man, but a man." Cash fired two slugs in the guys legs. "Arrrrggghhh!" Cash walked over to the bleeding screaming theif.

"So this what y'all want me to do huh? You wanna force my hand and make me off you for what? Why y'all fuckin up something good?" He swung his gun across his workers face. "I'm feedin y'all. Why steal nigga?" Cash kicked him in his ribs.

"Aaaarrrggghhh I'm sorry I fucked up! I was greedy!"

"Flamez c'mere bull!" Flamez went over to Cash who was standing over the bleeding worker. Cash face was full of rage he began to sweat heavy.

"This ya fault so handle it!" Cash handed him the gun. Flamez clutched the weapon and aimed it. "Do it!" Cash screamed at him.

BOC BOC BOC BOC!!! Flames squeezed off and left his target slumped and lifeless. J-jay had heard that it was some money coming up missing. He was the reason Cash had Thompson street, this was his hood. After the shots rang out in the spot he came in.

"Yo bull thats the nigga?" He asked looking at the stiff body on the floor.

"Yeah give his family 50 grand. J-jay make sure his family get the money please!!!"

"Yo bull I got it. Trust me!" Cash wanted to, but in this game you couldn't. The first time someone think they can get over, they will try their hand. He looked over at another one of his watchers who looked nervous.

"Yo you think if you had Flamez job you would of did some dumb shit like this?" The guy looked at Flamez who mean mugged him and then back at Cash. He was 22 and was loving the 5 grand a week. He was ballin for him.

"Naw bull!"

"Ard well we shall see that's ya position. This shit better run smooth. Check ya peoples and take care of them. Don't show no weakness or you will get tried. Then shit like dis dead nigga right here happen!"

"Yo bro what I'm a do if this nut ass nigga taking my job?"

"Gimmie my gun bull." Flamez passed the 40 to Cash.

"BOC BOC!!!" Flamez caught two shots to his legs.

"Cash don't do this bro! Cash dis me!" Flamez saw the look in Cash's face as he crawled on the floor bleeding from the knee caps. Cash put his hot barrel to Flamez forehead, then drug it down his cheek and in his mouth. "Everybody listen because this is very important. No shorts ever again in this room. You all have been warned it will not be tolerated. I pay too well for you to want extra! If you want to quit, bye you can leave now. Next time a dollar come up missing after today, everybody dies in this room."

Cash looked down at Flamez who still had the gun in his mouth.

"I fucks wit you bro you makin me look bad with this dumb shit. It's costing me money and that's like stealing from me anyway. You fired, McDonalds hiring. "Cash took the gun from his mouth and tossed it to J-jay.

"Get me another ratchet get rid of that! Ayo this ya block bro I know you can't see everybody but make sure the people you get to run these trap cribs is official.This my money! Ya'mean I got families to feed. Hold it down in here my nigga!"

"You already know!" J-jay replied with a new sense of focus. A dead body on the floor and a bleeding comrade will do that for you.

Cash left out the spot thinking of how his life had drastically changed. He was in a lifestyle where lives were took from violence and destroyed by drugs. He had a heavy hand in the community and he could really change the next generation. He had millions being generated he started thinking of new schools and rec centers in his name. He made a mental note to really give, even more than what he already had. This area was why he was extremely wealthy, why wouldn't he give back to it?

His mind drifted to the 7 carat yellow diamond ring he put on Dallas hand on her birthday. She cried tears of joy, he had his family and her family come to the house.He wanted her to be his wife, not just wifey. He didn't want any other woman to love but her and she deserved the lifestyle he provided. He wasn't getting any younger and life was short. He wasn't getting married until they were in Atlanta set up, but he was on a road to committing.

Cash thought about his best friend who was locked away. He would be home soon but he still missed his right hand. Through all the street activity he was there to back him up. Now he felt like a piece of him was gone. He wanted to get back behind the scene and have his homie hold it down. He thought that he wanted to be a boss,he dreamed of this since he was a kid. Cash just never realized the massive responsibility. Lives depended on him to survive, that's what made it hard to stop and walk away. It wasn't just him who was living good and surviving from his lifestyle, so it wasn't just that easy. He wanted to pass the crown…he was getting too old for this shit.

Cash drove through West Philly in a daze. He slid up Felton Street and realized how far he had come. This is where it all started, and it was just how he left it, dry. It wasn't a crack head in sight or a mob of guys on the corner serving. Kids were in the street having a good time playing catch. While the elder sat on the porch enjoying the day. They looked happy. "How are you doing Anthony?" A voice from behind said, as he leaned on his car watching the kids throw the football. He turned to see Ms. Mary, she use to babysit him when his mother was at work.

"Hey Ms. Mary.I'm good how are you?"

"I'm fine thanks to you."

"What I do?" He was confused but wanted to know how?veryone stop selling those drugs on the block. This area is back to normal before all that poison came in the neighborhood. There aren't lines of zombies trying to get high. It's peaceful again"

"Your welcome I guess." He never looked at it like that. He knew the block was hot and he had to set up shop somewhere else. He really saw how much power his word was at that moment. He looked around and the block did look peaceful. He smiled and was proud.

"What's good Cash?" We haven't seen you in forever." Tamara said from the porch. He walked over to the group of girls on the step gossiping he grew up with. All they did was sit there talk about the dopeboys, text and scroll through their social network pages like facebook. "Whassup with y'all whats new?" He asked the group of ladies.

"New is you pushing all this work out here where my check at?" Gloria blurted out.

"You got me confused I be chillin!" Cash said downplaying his million dollar drug empire. "Nigga please I heard you run West. You and my boo Rome got shit on lock!" Samone added, she use to mess with Rome and he always blessed her. She knew Cash was a boss out here. He was humble he always was like that.

"Y'all listen to people too much I be chillin I aint on it like that. People just talk babe!"

"So how you get that CTS and that Escalade, plus I seen you in a Range too! Nigga you got money stop fraudin, nigga this us. We watched you grow up!" Tamara said looking Cash in his eyes.

"I'm out but I holla at y'all be safe." Cash went in his pocket and eyes grew as his bankroll was revealed and it was all hundred dollar bills.

"Since I got West on lock as y'all say, let me look out," Cash joked and passed every one a couple hundred. He knew times were hard and people had kids to raise and bills to pay. At the end of the day these were his people. He always had a secret crush on Tamara and wanted to get at her, but he knew if she gave him play now it was because of the money and his status. He gave them hugs and was back to cruising the streets.

"Hello." Cash said picking up the call from his mother.

"Cash I have to talk to you baby!"

"Go head mom!"

"You know ya cousin Musa come home next week?"

"Oh shit that's my nigga mom. He use to always take with him when I was a kid, he like my favorite big cuz!"

"Well he coming home on Thursday. Please Cash, don't let him get back out here and caught up with you. That boy did 20 years. He can't afford it baby!"

"Mom he is a grown man. I can't stop what he do or want to do.He older than me!"

"I know, just try not to bring him around it that's all. He might relapse you know what I'm talking about boy!"

"Mom I will try but I know after all that time he don't want to be broke!" His mom got quiet she really was concerned about Musa, after a 20 year bid she feared he would come home and something bad was going to happen.

"Love you mom I gotta go!" Cash hung up and thought about the memories he had of Musa, but everyone called him Moose. His older cousin use to be a cold blooded gangster. He was from a different era so he was militant a former black panther. He use to get the community rowdy as a people and they would move for him. He went to prison for assault on a Police officer. They stopped him in traffic and told him to get out the car. The officer claimed Musa reached for something that's why he tazed him. Moose grabbed the cop and almost beat him to death. He sat there and waited for the ambulance and police. They gave him 20-40 when he was in his early 20's. Cash was going to make sure his cousin came home proper. He remembered in the 80's and early 90's when guys came home from jail his homies and family were prepared and looked out on money, clothes and even cars. Now a days you will be happy to get a welcome home from people. Cash wasn't going to have his people hold it down for 20 years and come home starving.

$ $ $ $ $ $ $ $ $ $ $ $ $ $ $ $ $

"Hello?" Dallas asked not recognizing the number that was calling her cell phone.

"I see you still got the same number!"

"Who is this I don't have time?"

"Your first!"

"Hey Twon, what the hell you want?"

"I wanna see you!"

"Boy I'm about to get married. I'm so over ya bum ass! How many baby momma's you got now?" Twon laughed, he had babies all over the city and didn't do shit for none of them.

"Eight but you drawin, we aint talkin about that. I just wanna." Click

Dallas didn't care who he was her man was Cash. They had been through hell and back again and wasn't no past dick long or good enough to jeopardise that. She called out for Cash but there wasn't a response. She went in the boy's room and he was snoring in Casheed's bed. She walked over to him and saw he was hard. She looked at her man and was proud. He was really trying and she saw the change since he put the ring on her finger. She went over to him and pulled his dick out. Cash was still knocked out and Dallas went to work. She slurped and gagged taking him all the way in her throat. Cash woke up feeling the sensation and a smile grew on his face when he saw the top of his woman head.

"Awwwwwww shit!" Cash moaned and Dallas gripped him with two hands and twirled on his penis like she was using a pepper grinder. She sucked hard and Cash exploded in her mouth.

"Shit!! Where that come from babe?"

"I just love you but I told you tell me when you nut I didn't wanna taste that nasty shit."

"Where it go then?"

"Where you think?" They both burst out in laughter. That's the kind of relationship they had that made them work. They had great sex, communicated and joke around. They were in love. Cash got a call from J-jay who told him he needed to come pick up some money. Cash got up kind of irritated, he had just got a good nut he was trying to chill. Money calls and business had to be handled. He got up and grabbed Dallas keys to the Escalade and was out the door.

Cash had made his mind up. When Rome come home he would exit smoothly and hand the whole operation off to Moose and him. He would move on to be a legit business man and club owner.

When Cash pulled up on Thompson Street everything was set up as usual when he came to get money. He would have his muscle stand outside with guns in hand just in case anybody tried to do a robbery. Cash didn't want to get too comfortable so he made sure he was cautious. He pulled up and his workers brought out three large trash bags full of money. J-jay came to the truck as Cash's crew loaded it up.

"What's the count J?"

"4.8," Cash looked like that had to be wrong. The number for this pick up was suppose to be 5.5, he didn't understand why is money was short.

"I took the 200 I was suppose to get, I put that money up for Rome, and then the money Moose getting bro. You know it aint no funny shit coming from this end," Cash forgot about the money he was taking out for Rome and Moose. He was going to do it big for his cousin welcome home party and Rome was his partner so his money was put aside every flip.

"Damn bull my bad I forgot about my people for a minute. I'm out, hold it down my nigga!" J-jay played his role as Cash's Lieutenant; he was getting more money than he ever did, so his loyalty was unconditional. Cash had put people in a better position to feed their family and do what they wanted in life. A very valuable rule to the game if you are a boss is to take care of your workers. You are as strong as your weakess link his former old head C.j use to tell him.

Cash sat at a red light on 52nd and Lancaster and noticed he was being followed. He wasn't about to lead his fans to where he stashed his money so he made a U turn to see if they really were on him. Just as he thought, he was being followed. The two crown Victoria cars made the same U-turn. As Cash looked at the two vehicles in pursuit he saw another Crown Vic pull in front of him out of nowhere. He came to a screeching hault to avoid the collision. Two guys with handguns hopped out pointing their weapons telling Cash get out the truck.

"Rome get locked up and now niggas just wanna try me huh! These niggas aint taking shit from me! I aint taking no loss!" Cash said as he reached under the seat for assistance. "Alright chill I'm getting out! Don't shoot!" Cash stepped out and let the automatic weapon sing. "BBBBDDDDDDDAAAAT BBBBDDDDDAAATTT!!!!"

Cash let a wave of gunfire loose and his adversaries were not quick enough to respond and caught the oncoming slugs. They flew back as the bullets ripped through their chest and opened it like heart surgery.

"BOC BOC BOC!!!"

"Ahhhhh shit!" Cash was hit he didn't know where, he just felt the burning sensation in his flesh. He took cover behind the front of the truck as the other shooters moved in from behind. His heart raced but he didn't feel scared he was more nervous. He put his arm out squeezing the trigger from the front of the Escalade. It was three masked men moving in after Cash let the weapon off.

“This my nigga right here, this how he do you huh?” One of the masked men said looking at his homie shot up and dead in the street. Cash heard someone say get the money. “BBBBDDDDDATTT BBBBDDDDAAT!!!”

Cash came from the other side of the truck and fired again. This time taking another two of them down. They hit the ground and Cash fired again to make sure they were dead.

“BOC BOC BOC!!!”

Cash was hit badly, he felt another bullet puncture him, then another. He tried to lift the Mac but it felt too heavy he dropped it. Then he fell to the ground bleeding. The remaining masked men walked up slow and was right in front of his face with the gun. Cash was sitting up against the passenger tire of the truck. The masked man kicked the Mac away and opened the back door of the truck.

“Don’t move nigga!” He told Cash who was fading out fast. He grabbed the bag from the truck and opened it up. “Jackpot!!” He saw all the stacks then went to reach for the other bags.

“BOOM!!! The sound of the shot gun brought Cash to reality. He was still seating there leaking bad. He saw the body slumped over in front of him with half his head blown off. He started to fade out again then thought of his money but couldn’t move.

“Cash Cash Ayo Cash wake up….”

He heard a voice and it was J-jay but he couldn’t talk he couldn’t respond. He wanted to say get my money, make sure you get the money.

"Call 911, call 911!!!" J-jay grabbed his bleeding friend and put him in the back of the truck. One of Cash's goons got behind the wheel.

"I got you bro…stay with me I got you!" Cash tried to speak and J-jay listened carefully as he held him close.

"Them niggas aint get no money…J they aint get my money tho." Cash whispered and passed out.

$ $ $ $ $ $ $ $ $ $ $ $ $ $ $ $ $

Cash had made it through surgery but had slipped in a coma. He took 5 bullets, three in the chest, and two in the stomach. The Doctor said it was a miracle he survived. It had been 2 weeks since the shooting and it was plastered over the news paper and on the news. The head line was. DRUG DEALER SURVIVED 5 SHOTS!

Dallas and the kids were by his side day and night. His mother and sister flew in and were supporting Dallas emotionally, but she was devastated. They gave him a 21% chance of surviving the surgery and when he went into the coma that made her panick.

When Moose came home he couldn't wait to see his little cousin all grown up. All the jails talked about were how Cash was running the city now, and getting more money than anyone. So Moose couldn't wait to fall in line and get this money. He was hurt when he came home and his family had all those tubes in him and was in a coma. He wanted to ride on whoever was responsible but no one knew anything. This hit came out of nowhere, but Moose hit the streets for answers. At 46 he was cut up like a bag of dope from many years of push ups and sit ups. He still had that militant mind set and it was only a matter of time before he hunted down the person responsible.

Cash finally awoke and it was like a long much needed nap. He felt rejuvenated until he tried to get up and then pain in his chest laid him back down. He began to snatch out the tube in his arm, and the rest of the things they had attached to his body. He looked over at Dallas who was sleep in a chair by his bed. He smiled, she was always there. He tried to re visit in his mind what had happened and flashes of gunfire, blood, the glass shattering and screams came to his mind. He saw the Mask man head get blown off and J-Jay and his boys come to the rescue. Then he thought of his money and the block and what he was missing. Did people think he was dead? Did they know he didn't go out like a nut he was busting his gun? A lot of questions he needed answered and staying in the hospital was out of the question for sure.

"Yo D wake ya ass up babe!" Cash shook Dallas and when she came to she thought she was still dreaming. Cash was fully dressed and ready to go like he didn't take 5 bullets two weeks ago that almost killed him.

"Cash what the hell you doing out the bed? And how you get dressed? You almost died where the hell you think you going? Get ya ass back in that bed!"

"I got shit to handle c'mon we out!" He needed answers and the streets had them, not the hospital. He checked himself out even against the Doctors wishes. He called j up and told him they needed a meet. So after dropping Dallas off, he headed to Thompson Street for the meet. Somebody had to tell him something.

$ $ $ $ $ $ $ $ $ $ $ $ $ $ $ $ $

"Whassup cousin?" Moose said as Cash came through the door of the spot. Cash looked at his family who was huge you could tell he had been locked up or in a body building contest. They hugged and Cash took a seat with his trusted street team all together.

"So what's been going on, how the block moving?" Cash looked at J-jay, Fat Mike then Moose and waited for an answer.

"Everything is everything lil cousin. I've been holding it down since that situation. Ya man J a real dude! I fucks with him.We got Thompson running like you never left."

"Good that's whassup. Moose I can't really be on the front line like I was. Rome booked and I'm beat up. I got to heal. Moose you playing Captain while I'm in recovery. Cuz this business it ain't personal. So keep this shit tight. You a O.G to this shit so I don't have to tell you how shit work. I need y'all niggas to hold it down while I fallback!"

"Lil cuz I hear you and I got you. I see you took them shots like a true G. Just heal up we got this."

Cash stood up and walked over to J-jay. "Good lookin my nigga for saving my life. If it wasn't for you bull they would of splattered my shit. Thank you bro!" Cash embraced him for a hug being appreciative on another chance at life.

"Nigga I told you I got you. I heard them first shots and me and the boys was on it! You already know!"

"So you aint even ask who put the hit out on you!" Fat Mike chimed in. Cash looked at him and hoped he had good news. All he wanted to do was put his gun to the coward who couldn't face him like a man and sent his bitches to do his dirty work.

"Who nigga?"

"Some South Philly nigga name Twon. I never heard of him but since the shooting he been bragging heavy and it came back to us." Cash thought about that name, he knew Twon. That bitch ass nigga tried to take him out over some pussy that he had years ago.

"I know that clown! That's Dallas first love, nut ass nigga! Let that shit die down don't touch bull yet, I want him to myself bro! I'm so serious." Cash got up and told his crew to hold it down and he was out the door headed home.

The kids were sleep and Dallas was waiting for him to walk through the door. When he saw her beautiful brown face and full lips he was proud that she would be his wife one day. Then he thought of Twon who had put a hit out on him over her, over something that wasn't his and hadn't been for years. He was confused he didn't understand that type of breed, who kills over pussy that isn't theirs? He really didn't know what kind of war he started…he was Cash from the West side. Somebody should of informed him Cash was up and active, and it was only a matter of time before he would catch up with him. When that day came it would be nothing but bloodshed.

"Baby I missed you, Cash I really thought someone took you from me! Baby I love you and when are you going to learn you can't do this shit forever?"

"Baby I'm here and as long as I got a breath in my body I will love you with all my heart. If you didn't already have that ring I would ask you to marry me again. I love you girl." Cash pulled his woman in tight and hugged her. His phone vibrated and he answered.

"You have a collect call from Rome. To accept dial 5 now to refuse this call hang up or dial 7 to block any further calls from this person. Cash quickly dialed 5 and heard his homie.

"Yo Dallas how my man holding up?" Rome sounded depressed he had been calling Cash's phone every day since he heard and Dallas would answer and tell him his status. Rome had already been in 3 fights since he got the news cash had got shot up. He was wrecking in the jail.

"This Cash nigga whats the deal bro?"

"Cash! Nigga don't you do that shit no more nigga!!! I thought I lost you bull, whats good? Ayo real shit my nigga its good to hear ya voice man I been wildin up here son."

"Son? Yo bull you been in New York too long you soundin like em." Cash joked.

"Yo bull you know when you around these niggas for so long that shit start to rub off. I been trashin niggas since I heard you was hit. Word up, any nigga that looked at me. I was on go! When I first heard I trashed the nigga who told me bull! I was buggin!"

"Yeah niggas tried me bro. Niggas really tried me If it wasn't for J-jay I would have been outta here!" They both were silent and soaked it in how real the situation was.

"Look the phone about to hang up bro I'm a hit ya jack tomorrow. You all I got Cash, you my brother. Be safe…when I get out I'm going to church bull. I wanna get saved bro!"

Click

The phone cut off and Cash laid back on the bed with Dallas on his chest listening to his heart beat.

"Two inches from my heart babe! Them pussies almost got me outta here."

"You here tho baby what you going to do with ya second chance is the million dollar question?"

Cash fell asleep with his mind in a hundred different directions. He thought if he would have died how would he be remembered? Would they say he was a boss, a real nigga, great father, or just another drug dealer or murderer? Would it have mattered if he took 5 with him but was gone too? He didn't want to be just another product of his environment. He wanted to be the person known for helping his people and trying to make everyone situation better. He wanted to be known as a man who took the world on and stood for what he believed in. Cash was groomed by the streets. He was battling with a cold heart and being human. The streets forced his hand to protect his self and take lives. These lives were people, and he couldn't take that back. These lives could not be returned or brought back because of his hand or word. Cash just wanted to live and living like he was, it wasn't going to be a long life.

Chapter 15

Lock Up

Rome had been down 11 months, he could of been home sooner in a halfway house, but he was maxing out. The fights caused sanctions so he was doing the whole year and a day in the jail. He knew it was time to go because he was getting use to jail and his daily routine. He woke up and worked out for 2 hrs, showered then ate. Depending on which C.O was on he would get some pussy and the rest of the day he gambled or read street novels. He never read on the street or finished school but he could read and count money like a professional. He was finding God in jail and began reading the Bible and the Quran. He also was working on his G.E.D and started rapping. He ended up being good at flowing.

He was into the book he was reading when he heard his name. He put the classic novel Charm City down by C.Flores and went outside his cell. He saw Steel talking shit to some guys about how he use to get money, just ask Rome. Steel was from his area but he didn't really know him well.

"You must don't know why they call me Steel nigga? When I hit niggas my fist feel like steel nigga. Don't play with me I ran shit on the street. Y'all niggas broke in here. I stay with money on my books!" Steel was tall 6'5 chubby muscular build with a big beard and bald head. Steel was playing poker and wasn't trying to pay what he owed. He knew if Rome was out there even if he didn't know him they both were from West Philly and he wouldn't let them jump him.

"You lost Steel just pay that bread, be fair nigga. You talking all this big money shit pay me mine!" Another inmate name Duce argued. Rome thought about his date tonight with his favorite C.O, Ms.Gamm. If something happened on the block they would be locked down and then he wouldn't be able to get some pussy.Hell no he thought and went to resolve the situation before it got ugly. Everybody on the block knew he had hands he already proved his self. That Philly nigga can fight!! That's what the C.O's and other inmates said.

"Whats poppin over here?" Rome said as Steel looked him in the eyes.

"This nigga owe some bread and he aint paying. If he aint paying we got problems. I don't care what they call him. I will put that steel in him he keep fuckin talkin!" Duce barked.

"Ayo Rome tell this nigga how Steel get down he better go head!"

"First off fuck outta here you drawin! You from my hood but I don't know you like that don't put me in ya shit. Pay what you owe baller!"

"What nigga I'm Steel! You better let these niggas know!"

"Listen Steel I heard about you but it wasn't for getting money. It was for sticking niggas! You use to say some corny ass shit like, just give it up nigga you don't want to feel the steel! Pay ya bread before bull smash ya big ass in here and I can't fuck my lil bitch and get my nut off!" Rome saw Redz walk up who was listening with his fist balled up.

"Hold up, you use to say that stupid shit? A nigga last summer got me for $2200, my chain and watch leaving the bar saying that bullshit! I'm a help you smash this nigga Duce!" Rome stepped in quickly.

"Hold up gangsta you aint helping nobody! He from my area as much as he a nut y'all aint gonna jump him. Shoot the one on one or we all just tear this bitch up!" Rome looked at Duce and Redz like, what y'all want to do?

"Aint no beef with us Rome we can shoot him a fair one! He pussy for real!" Redz said with confidence. He blew a kiss at Steel and winked at him.

"Go head Steel show them how much hard ya fist of steel are. Do you canon!"

Duce stepped up and he and Steel squared off.

"I'm a break ya fuckin face clown!" Duce said as he balled his fist tighter. BAM BAM BAM!!

"Arrgh!" Steel groaned as Duce hit him with a hard swift 3 piece. His lip split down the middle and it leaked blood. Rome started laughing and Steel got hype. Duce was 5'7 170lbs and Steel was just big for nothing. Duce went right back at it for another two to his chin and a hard right to the ribs bringing the big man to his knees. Everybody watched as Duce was connecting each blow with force.

"Get up nigga he beatin ya ass!" Rome heckled on the side line.

"Ahhhhhhhh!! Steel got up and rushed Duce. He picked him up and bear hugged him. Duce yelled in pain as Steel Sqeezed with all his might. "Ahhhrrgghh let me go nigga!! Why you grabbing me?"

"Shut up nigga!" Steel hit him with two vicious head butts to his face busting Duce nose open and chipping his tooth. He slammed him down hard and duce hit his head he was out. Steel got down and took advantage and pounded on his face. His fist was bloody he wiped them on Duce pants and stood up leaving him badly beaten.

"It's not gonna be that easy!" Redz said as Steel locked eyes with him and rushed. Red side stepped the attack and threw Steel head first into the steel bars. The top of his head split open and he passed out with blood pouring from his head. Redz looked at him and remembered his chain he loved so much he had spent 15 racks on it. He went over to Steel and started stomping his head to the floor even more.

"Bitch ass nigga. You fuckin fraud!!" Redz took one last stomp and walked off. Rome was right behind him.

"Yo bull let me holla at you!" Redz waited and Rome shook his hand.

"Real nigga shit you did ya thing I would of trashed him too! How much time you got left bull?"

"Something small like 3 weeks why whassup?" Redz asked curious, wondering why Rome wanted to know.

"Well when I get outta here I'm looking for some good soldiers. I like ya style, real nigga shit you know how my niggas move throw the name out there and see what you catch. Rome and Cash the niggas from West Philly who got it on smash. Yeah that's me! If you aint tryna be another nigga let me know! We get money!"

Over the next couple weeks Rome and Redz grew a relationship and Redz agreed he would be down with his team. Redz came in Rome cell and he was rolling up a joint.

"I'm sorry Lord for what I'm about to do and keep doing. Amen!" Rome was using Bible paper to roll his weed up. The next couple hours flew by and 6 joints later it was time for the 10pm count. Just as Rome expected it was Ms. Gamm and Mr. Smith counting. When Ms. Gamm passed his cell she winked and Rome instantly got hard. He didn't care if he paid for the pussy every time he hit, he had money to blow, so it was like the sex was free to him.

Hours later Rome awoke to a light in his face. He put up his hands to block the brightness of the flash light.

"Davis wake up you have court! Gotta take you downstairs." It was 4am, Rome got up halfway sleep, and he was cuffed. He was took to an office down the hall and uncuffed.

"Damn you took forever to come get me I fell asleep."

"I'm sorry baby I couldn't get away!"

"Well make it up to me." Rome pulled down his jail khakis and revealed his hard manhood. Ms Gamm got down on her knees and didn't hesitate. Rome held the back of her head as she sucked harder back and forth on his slammer. She went down to his balls then back to the dick real wet and sloppy with it.

"Yeah suck dat dick that's just how I like it! Damn!! Tell me you got a condom!"

"Yup!" She said ype coming off the tip of his dick and quickly pulling out the gold wrapper. Rome took the condom and quickly ripped it open and placed it over his penis.

"Take dat shit off and bend over I been waiting all day to buss ya ass!" She came out of her uniform pants and Rome gripped her neck and bent her over the desk.

"Take it slow baby don't try to beat it up like you usually do."

"Bitch please I ain't got time to make love. You gonna make that 500, I pay 250 if I take it slow?"

"Just do what you want Rome!" She said with an attitude.

"Right!" Rome jammed his dick deep inside her and began to stroke. Ms Gamm was one of the 6 females Rome was smashing. As long as you had money you could get whatever you wanted in jail.

"Awwwwwww Rome! RIGHT THERE!!" She came and Rome felt her juices slide down his leg. He started pounding long hard vicious strokes and she squirted loving every minute. Rome felt he was about to cum so he yanked out of her and snatched the condom off. "Get down, get down hurry up!!" Ms. Gamm got down and Rome jerked off in her mouth and let out a huge nut. "AWWWWWWWWWWWWW SHIT!!"

Rome laughed to his self and thought if this wasn't the life of a G what was? He was doing his time like a real man and still had his hands in the street. He ran the jail like the block. He and Cash had really made their way and it showed through the respect and love they received everywhere they went.

"Take me back to my cell shorty." Rome pulled up his pants and was to go.

"Damn boy you got some good dick! Keep fuckin me like dat and I might just fuck ya sexy ass for free. I came 3 times thank God!! Niggas is not doing me like dat in the

"I feel you this how it go. I'm Redz. What's ya name what you in for?"

"Twon from South Philly and some bullshit child support!"

That was only half the story. Twon was coming back from Harlem on his way to Philly with 5 bricks in the trunk. He was pulled over and he didn't know he had a warrant for child support in Philadelphia. The Police got him out the car and did a search and found the coke, they lock him up and now he was here talking to Redz.

"If you need some type of food or soap and shit go holla at Dot two cells down,he got the care packages my peoples put together for the homies or just official niggas. Soap, soups, chips, deodorant, it will hold you down until ya money good."

"Solid, good looking out!" Redz didn't think nothing of it, Twon was just in for child support. He went back to Rome's cell and told him the situation with Twon.

"Yo dude in here for child support!" Redz told Rome as he came in his cell while he was reading.

"Where he from who is he?"

"Twon from South Philly."

"I never heard of em. You tryna smoke?" Rome asked as he pulled out a sack of haze he got from another inmate.

It didn't take Twon long at all to get comfortable, after a couple days he was playing cards, chess and talking about his war stories on the street.

"I was about to be paid out there! Before I come in here I had a lick set up with my ex girl baby dad. This nigga was eattin heavy in my city. I get the word on a pick up.

Suppose to be crazy millions. I get the team to run down on him. This nigga lay all them niggas shit was crazy if I would of got away with it I would of went Cuba with my bread!" Twon looked around and a lot of people got quiet. The story was too familiar to Cash getting hit and everybody on the block new about Cash because of Rome.

"Why everybody looking at me like dat?" Twon saw Rome go to his cell then looked at Redz.

"You ran ya mouth too much plaboy!" Rome went in his cell and put 10 batteries in a sock, he had been waiting for this day! He came back creeping behind Twon while Redz talked to him. He swung the sock striking Twon on the side of the head. He turned to see it was Rome and caught another to his eye knocking him out. Rome stood over him and went across his head.

"Nigga is you stupid! You tried the wrong one! You see my hand nigga Cash my brother pussy!!" Rome cracked him again over the head and his face split and swelled up like a pumpkin from all the vicious blows. Redz came over and began to stop him as Cash repeatedly hit him with the sock full of batteries. Rome told Redz to fallback and pulled the shank from his boot. "Nigga whoever said you didn't get away with it? You did what nobody did. You lived to tell!!" Rome started stabbing away at Twon's stomach as blood squirted and he screamed in agony until he let out his last breath. Never did he imagine he would run into Cash's people in a New York jail. As his life slipped away he wished he could turn back the hands of time, because it wasn't worth the outcome.

When Twon's body was found stiff by the C.O's the jail went on lock down. Rome and a few others were sent to the hole for investigation. Rome was upset because he wasn't allowed food from commissary and no one down there had weed. It was cold but he was a soldier he knew this was procedure and nobody would rat him out without ending up like Twon. He received a letter from Redz who went home laws week, he only had a few days left. He wrote Rome and told him he would be waiting on him to get this paper.

Rome stood up as he heard the door to the tier he was on in the hole. It was trays and Rome was starving. He never ate the food from the jail he ordered on can'teen. Now he was on restriction so he had to result to the bull shit they served.

"Ayo Blizz let me get dat cake on ya tray bro? Tell the C.O pass dat!" Rome yelled down to one of the other inmates.

"I got you!"

How you doing sir, I have your meal." The female C.O said as she opened the metal slot to his cell. Rome grabbed his tray and looked at the petite darkskin woman with short hair. He could tell she had a nice ass because those uniform pants were hugging her hips.

"Damn baby you new or something I aint seen you before whats ya name?"

"Ms. McCoy."

"Nice to meet you and thanks for the food I love your attitude. They got you working the hole with all the goons huh. You scared?"

"No I'm fine I have been doing this for years I'm just new here. My girlfriend said this was the spot to work if I wanted some extra money."

“Who ya friend I might know her?”

“Ms. Gamm!” Rome smiled these female C.o’s were thirsty and when they acted thirsty he always gave them something to drink.

“Oh so she told you to holla at me huh? Well give the rest of these dudes they food I don’t want to hold nobody food up down here. Niggas starving! Come back whenever you ready I know she broke everything down already.”

“Yeah she said $1500!” MsMcCoy said excited.

“Nizz look I’m short I leave soon. I can give you 7 cuz I’m in the hole, if not it was nice speaking with you!” She thought about it for a minute and agreed to be back later tonight when people were sleep.

Rome was waiting patiently Ms.McCoy didn’t come back until 5 in the morning. Rome was on his bed already naked with his dick in his hand. She came in his cell eyeing his huge throbbing penis. “I see you already ready!” She began taking her clothes off. “Yeah I don’t play with it. You got a condom?”

“Yup!” She and Ms.Gamm had been talking about Rome all day she told Ms.McCoy he was a beast and it was worth it. She stood in front of Rome naked and he pulled her close and gripped up her fat ass. “Damn this jawn soft!” He pulled her down to her knees and she devoured his member with those soft lips. “Oh shit, shit, damn hold hold up!” Rome felt hisself about to nut but he had to hold back because he wanted to dive in the pussy. She was going up and down on his dick super fast and Rome was loving it.

"Chill you got me bout to nut. Let me see that condom and bend that ass over!" She passed him the condom and Rome got behind her round booty and spread her butt cheeks. She was already dripping wet and ready to fuck!

Chapter 16

Getting Right

Things with Cash physically were getting a lot better. His body was healing good and the team was holding him down. Rome was coming home today and things would be back to normal. The team was going to pick him up in style.

A year and a day had come and went. So much had happened during the time he was away in that short period. He missed his right hand man and his partner in crime. It was time to get his spot back and show the streets Rome was home!

"Davis you packed up your out of hear?" An officer said as Rome stood by his door awaiting his release.

"Yo bull just let me out I aint taking shit!" Rome went to get dressed Cash had sent his clothes in a day prior to his release.

"I hope I never see you motherfuckas again! Real rap!" He said as he finished getting dressed and was walking out the door to meet his freedom. When Rome stepped outside that jail he felt his legs get weak. He inhaled the fresh air and thanked his lord he was out. He saw Ms.Gamm and Ms.MCcoy outside smoking a cigeratte talking. He didn't see his boy anywhere. "Where ya people at it looks like you need a ride!" Ms.Gamm joked seeing Rome with the confused face. Loud music was heard coming from around the block and honking. "BEEP BEEP BEEP BEEP!!!"

"That's what I'm talking about. Take a look ladies. The crew pulled up just in time 3 cars deep. Cash was in Rome's Escalade with the 26 inch rims and the doors up blasting

Young Jeezy's Welcome Back. J-jay was behind Cash in Rome's Benz and Moose was in a black 745 Bmw. Cash hopped out first with a huge smile.

"My nigga, is that my fuckin right hand all husky on me?" Rome was 170 lbs when he went in, and now a solid ripped up 215lbs. Those push ups and sit ups did wonders to his build.

"You already know!" Rome said and embraced his team with hugs and handshakes. Cash handed him a stack of money. Rome looked at it and smiled. Cash was always there for him that was really his brother in his eyes.

"That's just 20 for ya pocket!"

"I hope you like this jawn I put my foot in it driving from Philly. Welcome home nigga!" Moose said referring to the Bmw.

"Ayo y'all my fuckin niggas. First off J-jay keep the Benz I heard you was there for my nigga when he needed you. So that's you! Y'all talkin bout me tho look at Moose. This nigga like a black Hulk!" Rome grabbed his arm feeling his muscle and they laughed. Just as they all were in the midst of laughter two Spanish girls got out the Benz in their underwear.

"You know it ain't right unless we got some hoes for you!" J-jay said as the girls kissed Rome on both his cheeks and hopped back in the car to avoid the chilly winds.

"Daaamn y'all niggas really looked out!" Rome looked back to see the looks on the tricking C.O's face.

"Oh shit y'all let me introduce the hoes! Them two right there dick suck on a million! They was bout they business. Say hi bitches!" The team looked at the salty face females and they got in their cars and were ready to go back across the bridge.

"He'll be back they always come back!" Ms. Gamm said with an attitude

$ $ $ $ $ $ $ $ $ $ $ $ $ $ $ $ $

The team pulled up on Thompson Street and parked up. They had a meeting but Cash knew his friend had to get his off first with the ladies.

"Ayo knock them hoes down and c'mon cuz we got business to discuss. You can fuck hoes any time. This some real talk we got to go over."

"Fuck these hoes I'm a fuck em but let's get business taken care of first. I be back I gotta go pick somebody up." They shook hands and Rome pulled off with the ladies in the back of his truck.

"Yo J-jay go get Tank tell him we got a meet Tell him today he getting a promotion!" Cash said and he and Moose went into the main spot where they discussed business. As the team piled in and sat in the living room Cash was puffing some Haze and waiting on Rome to return. J-jay, Moose, and Tank all sat there wondering what Cash was about to have the meeting about.

"So whassup Cash?" Tank said getting impatient. Tank was security apart of Cash's muscle on Thompson. He was about 6'2 300 pounds muscle. He was a live wire and ready to shoot on call, he never backed down from anyone and always was quick to pull the trigger. Cash saw loyalty in Tank and a lot of people feared him. So Cash knew he would be a good addition to the squad.

About 30 minutes later Rome came in with some lightskin pale face kid with braids that were light brown but gave a golden look off.

"Who the fuck is this?" Cash stood up and Tank pulled out his gun and aimed at the lightskin brother. When the gun came out everyone was in an uproar.

"Whoa whoa Tank put that shit away!" Rome barked.

"Put it away Tank…put it away." Cash said and Tank slowly put his gun back in his waist band. Rome was standing in front of Redz to protect him. "This my nigga Redz! He helped me wit that nigga Twon! Yeah I never told you bro, that nigga in a box now. He came through the jail bragging and shit. Me and my nigga got him the fuck outta here! This Redz and I promised him a seat at the table, he ready to put in work!" Cash couldn't believe his ears that Twon was dead. He had many dreams of putting his gun to that clown's face and blowing his head off. He really wanted to handle that personally but as long as that coward was gone Cash could find peace.

"If my nigga say you cool, then you cool with me! Good lookin on that situation!" He shook Redz hand and was ready for the meeting to begin.

"Everybody take a seat and let me break down the master plan to get us all filthy rich and out the game! We got me, Tank, Moose, J-jay, Fat Mike and now Redz. This the money team. Y'all mafuckas that's right here right now is it. We got our soldiers and workers but y'all the enforcers, the back bone to this shit workin." Cash looked around the room and everyone was listening carefully. "We about to really take this bitch over, and I'm not that greedy. I don't want the whole Philly that would really cause confusion. West Philly, where I was born and raised. I need this whole mafucka!"

"What that mean bull?" J-jay asked from the couch.

"That means everyone in West get they were from us! Every block that's moving work that should be our work they moving. I feel like this, we all can eat and ball hard. If these lil niggas wanna be broke and not get down with the winning team we go to war!"

"Ayo Cash you on some Nino Brown type shit!" Tank stated.

"Naw Thompson Street was some Nino brown type shit. We on some W.T.O shit, West Take over! I don't think we should have a problem the work the best in the city and im giving cheap so we can all eat. I know niggas aint got bricks they got packs or a lil 9 or half a bird. I will front every block birds and we get it. They cop from us and do they thing or work for us! Either way its more money than niggas been getting! Cash looked around the room for any uncertain facing so he could say his next proposal.

"Listen if niggas ain't with it I respect it. Niggas might get booked or die. But I thought you were dead any way if you broke. Let's get rich or die tryin cuz just living aint living to me!"

"I'm ridin!" Rome blurted out.

"True!" Fat Mike said.

"Look fellas if you not feeling it I got $300,000 for you to walk away right now. Nobody forcing ya hand, y'all family! So if you not with it take the money and keep it pushing, but you can't hustle no more, I'm paying you to get out the game or ride it out with us! All I can promise is while with W.T.O you going to get rich. Fillthy and all I ask is your loyalty, cuz I gave you an out!" Everyone seemed to be contemplating as cash just walked around the room speaking to his street team.

"The choice is yours! We ain't worrying about no cops I got the mayor in pocket for as long as I need him. 100,000 racks a month go to that cocksucker for keeping us below the radar. We W.T.O niggas and everybody bout to know us! So if you not with it, I got the bread right here I hope y'all be safe and make it off that."

"I can't do shit with 300 racks but blow it! Cash you already know how I get down. Let's get it!" Fat Mike added.

"Well since we all in it together let me give y'all something." Cash popped open his LV brief case on the coffee table. "These chains represent your commitment and dedication, hopefully y'all got a plan and when you ready to exit you can comfortably. I got a club in the making I'm going hard for a year with y'all and then I'm done. Moose and Rome are going to take over. I got kids I can't make this my life anymore." Cash began passing the chains around. They were platinum chains with the iced out W.T.O piece. "Redz I didn't know about you but it's a phone call so give me a few days."

"True dat it's cool!" Redz said checking out Rome's chain as he put it around his neck.

"Now next is the most important part. The Mayor himself came up with this to make it easy on his people and ours. We got license plates, W.T.O, whatever car you drive make sure you switch the plate to these and you won't get pulled by the locals. We just gotta go out here now and politic with these dope boys and see if they with it or wanna get lifted. Redz I say you go with Tank and y'all take 39th to 52nd and Moose and J-jay take 53 to 58th. Mike already got his section in line his niggas with it that whole area say they wanna eat." Cash passed out the license plates but was short one for Redz and said tomorrow he should have one first thing in the morning.

"Fellas let's hit these streets bring the work with y'all, put them plates on, and you already know, strap up. We can ride dirty!!

$ $ $ $ $ $ $ $ $ $ $ $ $ $ $ $ $

W.T.O hit the streets hard the following week was meetings, and roll ups on the West Philly drug dealers. W.T.O had a plan and they set out to accomplish it. If your block sold drugs or if you were a known drug dealer you needed they work or you couldn't work. You could move or operation to another part or get this money. Everyone basically was with it why not, they saw how Cash was moving and he was really trying to get everyone to eat and get money from his area. He grew up poor and his area was low class. This was poverty he seen people do bad things when they needed to pay a bill or provide for their children. His thoughts were, if everyone was living there comfortable it wouldn't be so much tension and hunger to cause violence. The next generation might see peace and a good living. He wanted his children to never want for anything and live like the Cosby kids. Until growing up he realized that was just T.V and then he was introduced to the game.

Cash floated through West and went through Felton Street. Every time he was alone and his mind drifted it always brought him back to this block. He saw lil Omar sitting on his steps so he parked, this was the next generation right here he wanted to see where the kid mind was at. He got out and approached him.

"Whassup youngbull what you doing out here?"

"Chillin waitin on you for real for real!"

"Why?"

"I want you to put me on Cash, I wanna be a gangster like you. You getting money you killed them niggas who shot you came back and still here getting money! These oldheads fucked up out here! Niggas broke I need to eat!" Cash looked at the 14 year old and couldn't believe his ears. This sounded like him years ago with C.j.

"Naw don't be like me or nobody. You don't want to be no gangster that's for damn sure lil nigga! They die or go to jail that's it. No get chubby and move to Miami these niggas check the fuck out or get 100 yrs! You want 100 years youngbull?"

"Nizz!!"

"Look at this nut shit!" Cash pulled up his shirt showing his bullet wounds that almost ended his life. "You don't wanna live like this I gotta watch my back everyday and stay strapped! People wanna kill me,rob me,tell on me, lock me up! This shit real but niggas don't tell y'all that they just give y'all work! Ayo go to school so you can be a boss or chase ya dreams. Here!" Cash went in his pocket and gave youngbull everything he had.

"Here this what you want me to put you on for, so you can get money. Take it take all that shit. Maybe it will save ya life." Omar eyes were out of his head, Cash really gave him everything he had in his pocket. He was speechless he didn't even say thank you as Cash hopped in his car and peeled off. He had just got $22,000 all hundreds for free.

"I'm going to the studio!!" Lil Omar said with a huge smile and ran in the house.

Chapter 17

Still Grinding

Moose was at the spot on Thompson going hard in the cocaine. He was snorting line after line. He was sweating and his eyes were wide, he was high as a g4 jet. Rome walked in and seen Moose with his nose in a pile of coke.

"Damn nigga slow down on that shit!" Rome warned him.

"I'm grown nigga I do what I want!" Moose added with authority.

"My bad O.G, I don't want ya big ass flippin out on me! Do you I'm just saying that shit pure as shit that aint no cut up bullshit that's like 91% nigga! Next thing you kknow you gonna be smoking and then it's a rap kill yaself. You can't be no fiend out here bro! Leave that shit alone!"

"What? I got this I just party here and there. Nigga I been doing this since the 80's I'm cool!" Moose phone rang and he answered.

"Yo!"

"We got problems!"

"Come thru!"

"5 minutes away!!" Click

"Who was that?" Rome asked.

"J-jay said we got problems!"

J came through the door with Flea. He was from North Philly and Rome fronted him 2 birds to test the waters and see how Erie ave move and maybe they could do business. Flea had fucked the money up then Rome fronted him 2 more because he thought he would make it right. Now the money was short when J came to pick up but Flea didn't have no more coke. It didn't add up.

"Whoa J what happened with Flea? I know that money straight I put 4 birds in ya hands in the last 3 weeks." Rome said as he sttod up from the arm of the couch and whipped his gun out.

"This nigga gave me 5 grand and said he aint got no more work he got robbed! I said nizz canon we out!" J-jay explained.

"Flea what the fuck you doing smoking my shit or you tryna get me!?" Rome went across his face with the gun bringing Flea to his knees.

"Arrrrggghhh!!! I swear to God man I will get the money. I got robbed tryna sell some South Philly nigga a jawn for 30! I thought I could get him!"

"Naw canon you tryna play me you think I'm soft bull? You really tryna fuckin play me?"

"BOC BOC!!"

Rome shot him in both hands and then back smacked him with the gun.

"AHHHHHHHHHHHHHHHHHHHHHH!!!" Rome walked over and put the gun to his head.

"Chill Rome chill!!" Moose pulled his arm down before he sqeezed the trigger. He had a better idea. "Let me talk to handle bull. I think B.B will make him tell the truth .She always get niggas to talk." Moose went in the kitchen and appeared with a bat. Rome just shook his head and laughed.

"Hold up real quick." Moose snorted another line and then clutched the bat.

"I call this B.B cuz it's a bad bitch. A nigga never lied once he saw it and definitely never lied again when he felt it. So whassup you tryna play us nigga?" Moose eyes were blood shot read and he lifted the bat in the air.

"I swear to God my nigga ard my babymom took that shit and left the city with some nigga. I'm not lying!" Flea begged as he cried and pleaded for his life.

"I believe you. I do....tie this nigga up J!" J-Jay tied Flea to a chair his hands were still leaking blood and the side of his face was swollen like a football. "Listen I cracked a lot of heads with this jawn bull! It aint crack yet. I love crackin niggas heads from North tho. Y'all niggas think y'all hard.You think we going for that nut ass story?" Moose swung the bat cracking Flea's knee shattering his bone.

"Ahhhhhhhhhhhhhhhhhhhhhhhhhhhh!!!!" I got robbed I swear to God!"

"I thought your baby mom took it nigga! See!" He swung again doing the same to his other knee. "Ahhhhhhhhhhhhhhhhhhhhhhhhhhhhhhhh!!" Flea was in severe pain he cried until the shots to his head muted his existence.

"BOC BOC!!"

"Ard fuck that shit get this nigga outta here you wanna play with him." Rome passed his gun to J-jay and left them. After J-jay and Fat mike got rid of the body Moose was left alone with his bloody bat and pile of coke. He sniffed another line and dialed a number.

"Ayo Juicy whassup I need to see you tonight!"

"I'm good baby! You rather fill ya nose then fill this pussy. Your dick barely get hard anymore I aint with sucking dick for 2 hours boo! You got me the last 3 times like that. Call when you slow down on that shit!" Click

Juicy hung up in his ear and Moose was shocked. He slammed down his phone and broke it. "Fuck them bitches!!!" He snorted another line and grabbed his crotch. Before he knew it he was out like a light.

Tank came back and saw Moose sleep in a pile of coke with the bloody bat in his hand. Tank shook his head and called Cash.

"Yo bull ya cuz on that white girl hard he need to chill."

"What you mean hard?"

"All day everyday! You need to holla at him maybe he might listen to you."

"True good looking bro!" Cash didn't like that at all. They were in this game to get money not high. Moose was using the product they sold, a crucial rule to the game he violated.

$ $ $ $ $ $ $ $ $ $ $ $ $ $ $ $ $

When Cash came in the spot down Thompson Moose was still sleep.

"Look at this nigga!" He was disappointed in his older cousin he was snoring loudly with his face in a pile of white powder. He smacked Moose across the face and he jumped up surprised from the stinging sensation on his cheek.

"Yo cuz why the fuck you smack me nigga?"

"We got to talk fam, you fucking up!!"

"Nigga first of all I'm living my life. I spent 20 fuckin years and 9 months in jail not you or none of these other lil niggas! Me! I'm 46 cuz, if this what I wanna do nigga this what I'm a do. I'm grown!"

"I was gonna talk you out of doing it but you right. You grown, you did 20 years. Fuck that! You wanna play catch up and get caught up. I told you cuz, this business! You snorting my shit up, on my time, in my fuckin spot!" Moose looked at Tank who was smoking a cigarette on the love seat. He knew he prolly called Moose and ratted him out and he didn't like that. If you would tell about that you would tell about anything he thought. He promised to play Tank closer.

"Is you listening nigga?" Cash took him out of his trance.

"Cuz my fault, I will get this shit together mybad!" Cash looked at him in his eyes and just left without saying anything.

On the ride back home his mind was on his club then he got a call and it felt like fate.

"Mr. Miller the property is ready it will be available for the grand opening this weekend congratulations!" Cash was so proud his dream was finally done. He was going to celebrate with the team and start getting that legal money.

"Thank you i appreciate that." Cash flew home he couldn't wait to tell Dallas the good news.

$ $ $ $ $ $ $ $ $ $ $ $ $ $ $ $

"Listen up listen up!" Cash held a bottle of Rose in his hand, this was his second bottle. "We gonna go in that jawn and shut shit down and let these nigga know we in here. W.T.O nigga!! My club done I'm done with this bullshi,t I got one in Atlanta, and I'm a have one in every major city. Big money boss shit!" Cash looked at his team in front of him at the spot. Everyone was fresh to death and ready to shut down 8th Street Lounge. They had all the lil homies riding too all of them had W.T.O shirts on. They were going to show up 100 deep easy tonight. Everybody with two bottles.

He was on already from the pills and weed and now he was sipping champagne before they even got to the club.

The W.T.O team pulled up at 8th street Lounge too many cars deep. The front line was Cash in his Range Rover, Rome was in the Escalade, Tank was in the Hummer H2, J-jay was in the Benz and Moose and Redz were both in Tahoe's full of the goons. Plus it was cars behind them, they came to turn up.

When W.T.O came in heads turned, people moved some left and others just watched in amazement. Cash ordered 100 bottles to start everybody off with. It was packed and all the young hot girls were picking and choosing.

"You already know what it is when W.T.O step in the spot. I see you Cash I see you Rome we know who getting money!" The dj said over the mic and dropped Freeway's hit single, What we do. When that song came on in Philly it just did something to the crowd, it was a classic song out of the city. Everyone was having a good time they had V.I.P over crowded, and the whole W.T.O held bottles in the air and bounced to the music. It really looked like a rap video. Only thing was this was real life.

"I heard about you! You suppose to be like the king of the streets! My whole hood knows about you!" Cash was sitting between two thick young pretty ladies. One was in one ear and one was in the other. He listened to both of them stroke his ego.

"Don't believe everything you hear I'm just a club owner I don't be in the streets!" He turned to the other girl who had his chain in her hand in amazement.

"This jawn heavy! Is it real you know niggas be fraudin like that rapper bull Frank Flush, you heard of him. He suppose to be from West with all the fake jewelry?"

"Trust me this aint fake baby. This cost me 250 just for the piece." He bragged and noticed Rome getting some head in the corner. He smiled at how wild his homie was.

"Yizzo another 100 bottles this shit real over here!! We in here, these niggas aint fuckin wit us! What?!!!" Cash yelled, he was so high and drunk he didn't even realize one of the girl's he was sitting between had took his hand and had it in her pussy.

"Me and my girlfriend wanna be W.T.O girls can you get us in?" She said and pushed his fingers deeper inside herself.

"I'm about to get married ladies I'm sorry a nigga tryna be good!" He said and removed his hand from her wetness. "I be back tho!" He got up and wiped his hand on her dress nonchalantly. He made his way to the bathroom to wash his hands and get his self together, he was really intoxicated. As he went toward the restroom he saw Redz grinding on a big booty, she was looking like Serena Williams was in the club from behind.

$ $ $ $ $ $ $ $ $ $ $ $ $ $ $ $ $

“Damn baby that ass soft as shit you know you dancing with a real nigga right?” Redz asked the big booty goddess.

“You with W.T.O I see ya chain. Y’all niggas getting money! You cute whats ya name?”

“Redz I seen you cuffed up with that lame earliar about to he let you free. Who was dat?”

“That was my ex he don’t get the picture it’s over. He cheated on me with some dirty ass girl from south west ewwww that nigga a flea!”

“Well c’mon lets go to V.I.P we got that shit on smash!”

$ $ $ $ $ $ $ $ $ $ $ $ $ $ $ $

“Damn my nigga you too high right now!” Cash said to his self as he looked in the mirror at his blood shot eyes and threw water on his face. When he looked back in the mirror he saw a woman and then she was gone. He shook his head and splashed some more water on his face.

“What the fuck?!!” Cash saw Headz girl with blood coming down her face and he could see the bullet hole. She stood there looking at him in the mirror. She pointed at him.

“Ayo shorty ass stupid bull I’m fucking her tonight real shit!” A guy came in the bathroom with his friend and Cash looked in the mirror and she was gone. He went into the stall and tossed the last 6 pills he had. He was done with them, every time he popped those he started seeing things. That woman had been coming to see Cash ever since he started doing pills. He thought about that night and it was so vivid. He saw himself squeezing the trigger on the lady, than hearing the cries of the boys, and going up to their room. He was about to do it, his hand trembled and he began to sweat. He just couldn't pull the trigger. He left out praying someone would give his kids a pass like he gave if the situation ever presented itself. He came out the bathroom feeling a little better and walked toward the V.I.P.

"Nigga why you all up on my bitch?" Someone yelled and Cash saw some tall guy approach Redz real aggressive. Cash noticed the goons were on it and slowly were blending in the crowd getting closer.

"I ain't tryna marry the bitch chill bull. She already told me you old news so step off I'm helping you!"

"What nigga?!" He swung and hit Redz in the nose hard knocking him backwards and blood ran down his lips. The angry ex snatched his chain while he was falling backwards and slapped big booty across her face. Before she could scream he was being beat on by 20 dudes with W.T.O shirts, the club got rowdy and a free for all broke out from the mayhem. As usual the club ended with gun shots. One of W.T.O boys had shot somebody and everyone went for the door. Cash grabbed Redz but he pulled away. "That pussy snatched my chain!" Redz went over to the beaten body that was unconscious. He saw his chain on the floor by the bar. "W.T.O bitch I tried to warn you!"

Redz spit on the body and put his chain on. "This mine nigga!" He ran out the club and seen the cops pulling up. They had got there fast.

"Freeze!!!" They all had their weapons drawn.

"My bad officers I don't know what's going on in there, I was tripped and stepped on, you see me bleeding." The officer saw the W.T.O chain around his neck and spoke up.

"Hold your fire! Don't shoot hold your fire! He's good!" He had received the memo W.T.O members were off limits. His check had $2500 more in it every other week because of these guys. They were cool with him. He had no problem looking the other way. He didn't see nothing and a lot of officers felt the same way. This was a direct order from the Mayor.

"You guys have a good night!" Redz saluted the officers and was out.

Chapter 18

Part Time Boss

Cash and Rome were slowly getting out of the spot light. It was too much drama in the streets and everyone was talking about W.T.O. Cash let Moose make all the major moves but J-jay was right there to back him up. Cash still was skeptical about Moose's coke habit, he hadn't slowed down not one bit. He told J-jay to keep a close eye on him. Moose was the active boss so if he said move the team moved. Now that the whole West Philadelphia drug trade was coming through W.T.O Moose was ready to expand. He was about to do what Cash thought was impossible, take the rest of Philly like they did West.

"Ayo Tank make sure we got extra clips cuz if these niggas act like they not tryna get our work. We squeezing on these sucker ass niggas!" Moose told Tank as he loaded up the H2 and they headed to South West Philadelphia.

"Yo bull you really going to do this? Cash said we run West and eat, you tryna draw!" Moose didn't care how big Tank was, he was trained to go.

"Look nigga we about to take the whole fuckin Philly over. We got the best work stop bitchin, unless you wanna find another job nigga!" Moose looked Tank in the eyes he really wanted to beat Tank ass for calling Cash on him. He still was holding that against Tank. Redz seen the tension between the two and interjected. "Yo bull we at least should get some soldiers to come with us. It's 3 of us bout to go holla at this bull and his peoples!" Redz suggested from the back seat.

"I really don't care if we got West or the whole city as long as I ball like I've been ballin. I don't give a fuck I'm ridin, but let's be smart." Moose went under his seat and pulled the dessert eagle out.

"I think we good! Yeah us 3 and all our bitches. We out!" Moose peeled off and they headed toward South west 55th and Greenway area. Some young dude by the name Streetz was known to have it in, and run his little section. Moose wanted parts.

$ $ $ $ $ $ $ $ $ $ $ $ $ $ $ $ $

Over in South West Streetz was leaning on his Range Rover, it was dark green with the matching rims. He was stunting at 24 he was moving 4 bricks and had 3 blocks doing numbers in his area. He just came home from an attempted murder so everybody knew he played with them guns. The best thing Streetz had going for him was he had a team full of young goons from15 to 19 putting people under, and they was on call. They had no picks.

"Why you play so much Danielle I need dat. I been waiting forever! Ya hair long as shit you killin these bitches boo!" Streetz spit his game to a young model type light skin girl name Danielle, he always wanted to fuck. She had let him taste the pussy a few times and he cut a few checks but she was a virgin at 18 or that's what he believed. She told him that to get money out of him she knew how Streetz got down. She was from the hood she was doing the same thing men been doing to females for years…lying!

"Baby I got you. Can I get some money to get my hair done? I wanna go to K.O.P later with my sisters too!" Streetz looked back his two homies who were sitting in his truck playing the Xbox he had installed. They weren't paying attention at all.

"I got you, you know you my boo! Ayo can I come get you later?" She almost laughed but had to hold it in as he passed her off $1500 like it was $15. She knew how niggas change up when they got the pussy, so she was going to milk him dry. When she put the money in her Gucci bag that he got her the other day she saw an H2 pulling up with the W.T.O tags. She wondered what they were doing out here. Then they stopped right beside her and she saw a gun. "AHHHHHHH!!"

"Chill shorty this ain't got nothing to do with you keep walking." Redz said as he and Tank hung out the window of the H2 pointing an Ak-47 and a Mac 10. Streetz was caught slipping as he watched Danielle walk off. Moose hopped out the truck wiping his nose. His gun was tucked but it was visible.

"Yoooooo what the fuck is this?" Redz got out first then Tank followed. The two in the back of Streetz Range Rover had their hands up.

"Damn bull you out here slipping. Niggas roll right up on you where ya muscle? Where them niggas that's suppose to see that before it come? Where your organization at bull?" Moose looked at Streetz and saw he was strapped and took his gun and tucked it with his.

"I don't know... niggas on call tho for sure!" Streetz said with a mixture of confidence and fear. He just wanted to see another day he heard of W.T.O.

"On call tho for sure, what you said that to sound like a g? Let me holla at you youngen I wanna put some money in ya pocket. Y'all niggas chill." Moose and Streetz walked around the block as Tank and Redz checked the two in the back of the Range who were holding their hands up. Tank aimed and Redz searched.

“Oh shit bull I know you, you that rapper bull Reed Dollaz I fucks with ya shit.” Redz said as he patted the rapper down and his homie. He took a 40 off of him and started back talking to the rapper.

“Yeah you heard of W.T.O right?”

“Yeah I heard y'all snappin out here. My man from West, G Buckz real nigga!”

“Oh shit that's my man! Hopefully dis nigga Streetz take this deal and get money with us. My peoples be drawin! Ayo you murdered that Either beat bull real shit! I ain't a hater!”

“Good look bro,” the rapper said and saw Streetz coming around the corner with Moose who was carrying a Nike bag. Moose opened the back seat of the H2 and put the Nike bag in, and pulled the black duffel out. He tossed it in the back seat of the Range landing on the guy's lap. It was ten bricks. Redz looked at the rapper and he looked back at him.

“Ya man took the deal, he smart!” Moose gave Streetz back his gun and Redz gave the young kid next to the rapper his. W.T.O had made an alliance and peeled off.

“Y'all niggas cool? That nigga said 17 a jawn I'm payin 25 I had to!” Streetz looked back at his homies who were just shocked at the entire situation.

$ $ $ $ $ $ $ $ $ $ $ $ $ $ $ $ $

Moose was snorting a line when he saw Cash number pop up on his phone. He was zooted he picked up the phone anyway.

“Yo cccuz.” Moose stuttered.

"Ayo me and Rome gotta shoot to Atl and see about my club, we prolly be gone for a week or so. Keep ya head on straight cuz!"

"I got this shit cuz!! Watch how I move bull." He hung up and went back for another line. What his cousin didn't know, Moose was hurting inside. His life had passed him by he had missed so much. Everyone he grew up with was dead or in jail. He had no friends, no people he grew up with or went to school with were around. He felt alone. He thought of his long nights in prison and being in jail when his mom died, then his father, he never had children. The powder made him numb and that's what caged the anger and frustration that made him violent. He just wanted to find peace and the only thing that helped him get close to that was the cocaine.

$ $ $ $ $ $ $ $ $ $ $ $ $ $ $ $ $

"Yo Streetz whassup we aint heard from you son?" Streetz knew he was going to get this call it was his connect from New York before he got connected with Moose and W.T.O. Moose ensured him that first day if he did work with him, when these New York dudes come through beefing he was riding. Moose promised it wouldn't be a problem. They was beating Streetz in the head for 25 a bird Moose was blessing him.

"Yeah bull I'm chillin I'm linked up with my peoples from the city." Streetz said confidently. "Yo son don't tell me them W.T.O niggas because you going to be like the third nigga that told me that shit son. What the fuck!?"

"Yeah that's my team now!"

"Y'all niggas funny! Real funny Streetz. So we done like that son?"

"Yo bull my peoples blessing me!"

"Man fuck ya peoples son! I'm on my way there Friday. Introduce me! I need to discuss business. Set it up. And Streetz don't try to fuckin play me, real shit son word up! I will smack ya kufi off nigga! Word to mother!" Click

"See I knew this was going to happen. These niggas know where I live!" Streetz had been dealing with his New York supply for 4 years and he knew a few other people they were also serving in the city. Steetz dialed Moose up he had to back his words now.

$ $ $ $ $ $ $ $ $ $ $ $ $ $ $

J-jay walked in the spot and Moose was on the phone. He had heard about the move he made with Streetz and didn't think it was a good idea. He just listened until he got off the phone.

"Ayo bull I told you I got you stop bitchin! Stop bitchin! You know the difference between a gangster and a hard nigga? A Gangster will die for this shit! Set it up and let me do the rest!" Moose hung up with Streetz who had just told him his New York supply wanted a meet. He wasn't worried at all.

"So why you fuckin with this nigga Streetz? You don't know bull you drawin!" J-jay asked looking at Moose to see his motive. He didn't understand why he was trying to risk something that could possibly jeopardize their movement. The operation ran smooth in West like clockwork.

"I'm expanding our business. When Cash get back he will be cool with it. So relax I got everything under control. I'm running this show just sit on the boat.Try some of this shit." Moose made a line for J on the table to snort.

"I'm good brother I don't fuck around."

The meet was set up for Friday and W.T.O team informed the New York supply of an old warehouse on the outside the city to discuss business. Moose was built for this and business was to be made. Who wouldn't want more money than they are currently receiving? W.T.O were all scattered throughout the warehouse armed and outside also the front and back of the warehouse. They were here for business, but if beef was what they want, it was on the menu as well.

Streetz pulled up with two Denali trucks behind him tinted out with New York plates.

Everyone was on guard no one knew what to expect from either side. Streetz and about ten New Yorkers got out. The W.T.O front line stood tall.

"Streetz y'all like 15 minutes late that's bad business," Moose said.

"Had to make sure it was business I don't need nobody to speak for me. You must be the person I need to see. I'm Frenchy fom 140th in Harlem." He extended his hand for Moose to shake it.

"Moose, nice to meet you. But my niggas gotta take all y'all gats if its business you shouldn't mind." He shook his hand and gave him a firm tight shake. Frenchy shook his head and told his people to put all the guns on the hood of the car they weren't giving them up.

"So what can I do for you French?" Moose asked as W.T.O and the New Yorkers were in a starring contest. The tension was thick so Moose told Frenchy to take a walk with him.

"Again, without everyone in our business whassup?"

"I wanna see who work better, prices better then mine I want in that's all. No bullshit I keep hearing about you guys even up New York. When I come to Philly I'm losing customers because W.T.O got the best work and prices! I'm eating I'm good, but if I can eat more fuck it son!" Moose felt like Frenchy was honest and another alliance would strengthen his empire because Cash was done, and Rome was right behind him.

"So what you getting your shit for French I know you was hitting Streetz in the head?"

"I grab from my peoples 20 to 30 for 16 and he front me whatever I get! So I buy 20 at 16 he give me another 20, and I hit him on the next flip. Now you telling me you can get it to me cheaper than my poppy?"

"I can tell you this if you ready to step it up to 100 because it got to be worth it bull. Niggas in my city grab 20 and I know them. You a risk I don't know you. So make it worth it and grab 100, I give em to you for 12."

"Word up, I respect that. Let me get a couple days to grab that bread and we can do business. I need that number son and with that shit you got I'm a kill these bird ass niggas!" They shook hands and Moose had made a valuable partner, and W.T.O placed their foot prints in New York. They were going global.

Chapter 19

Club Faith

In Atlanta, Cash and Rome were finally seeing the club done and ready for the public to come through the doors. Cash's lawyer had some papers made that documented an inheritance Cash received from a wealthy great uncle from Florida. So his club was in his own name and legit. Now it was time to let the people enjoy his vision.

Club Faith was luxury entertainment at its finest. It was a 3 story building. A bar on each floor, two cages hanging from the ceiling, they will be occupied with beautiful models dancing in them all night. The dance floor was glass, and under were tiger striped sharks he had imported for his customers to dance on. Flat screens were everywhere showing each floor. The D.j both had a huge flat screen behind it that showed outside which was downtown Atlanta. Cash had a stage for the performers he would have come through and bless it. His vision was right here in front of his eyes.

"Yeah Rome we bout to kill em! This shit gonna pop!" Cash said to his homie as they both stood in the Owners office on the third floor looking down at the club from the glass window.

"I know bull but you really done yo?" Rome asked sincerely.

"Yeah bro, I'm tryna live to enjoy all this chicken."

"I hear you bro but we got the city in our hands you think you can just give it away?" Cash looked him in his eyes then back down at his empty club.

"I think so."

Saturday came and it was the grand opening to Club Faith. Cash had hired his staff and had to have the finest and top of the line ladies Atlanta had to offer, working for him. He knew ladies attracted the guys and the guys spent money. Cash had hired the Magic City girl's from back in the day when he and Rome took the trip before. Kevalena, Tonja, and Diamond were barmaids and he knew they would entice the ballers to buy bottles. Cash had the radio promoting the grand opening and he had a few local celebrities coming through from the A.

Cash and Rome pulled up in front of the club in matching black Bentley G.T's. People and cars flooded the streets to get inside the new hot spot. The cameras were flashing and the red carpet was rolled out. As the cameras snapped Cash and Rome stood in front of the Club Faith advertisement and posed on the carpet. The crowd started going crazy when T.I and Tiny stepped out the back of the Phantom. They walked on the carpet to pose for the cameras as well. Young jeezy was in the building on stage performing already. So it was a mad house in the club with all the ladies at the stage.

The inside was packed they had to stop letting people in before the fire marshall was called. Young Jeezy finished his song and Cash went to the D.j booth and grabbed the microphone.

"How's everybody doing tonight? I see y'all looking real good, Atl getting money!!" Cash said and the crowd went wild. "I'm the owner my name is Cash, I wanna thank everybody for showing up tonight! I hope you enjoy yourself and let's continue to support each other coming up out the slums. We all were hungry and tryna get out the situation we were in, and achieve a positive outcome, and give our kids what we didn't.

Let's get this party started, thank you!" He raised his bottle of Patron in the air and the D.j played Ain't I by young L.A.

"Cash it's crazy in here! Look at V.I.P already on the second level." Kevalena shouted in Cash's ear.

"That's good, what's the problem?" He looked at Kevalena who had a short belly shirt that said ClubFaith on the front and staff on the back. She had some short shorts on that showed off her round bubble. Cash licked his lips remembering how wet her pussy was.

"B.M.F up there Cash!"

"Who dat?" Cash didn't know about B.M.F(Black Mafia Family) but once he heard the order for 200 bottles from the V.I.P section they were in, he was glad they were there.

It was really crowded as Cash made his way through the people. He felt someone grab his arm and looked back and saw the older woman Felicia from yesterday when Cash and Rome passed out flyers for the grand opening. He saw her and couldn't believe how beautiful and curvy she was. At 35 she didn't look a day over 22 and her ass was fat and juicy.

"Hey I was looking for you it's crazy in here." Cash shouted in her ear over the music.

"Follow me to my office and let's have a drink!" He held her hand and she followed closely behind as he lead the way.

"It's hectic out there! Take a seat and enjoy yourself. What are you drinking?" He said when they came through the door of his office. She looked around in awe at his style.

“Champagne is fine.” She looked down at the carpet in his over and the huge LV logos made her curious. “Is this a real Louis Vuitton carpet?”

“C’mon baby do I look like a nigga that would have some fake shit in here. Take ya shoes off and relax enjoy the view. Cash hit the remote and the curtains opened to give a great view of downtown Atlanta. Felicia kicked her heels off and sat on the soft brown leather sectional.

“This is soooo beautiful.” Cash handed her a glass of champagne and sat beside her and was amazed at her beauty. Her glasses just made her extra sexy. “All those young girls were down there talking about you. They want them some Cash and you up here with me. What you want with an old woman such as myself?”

“Listen them bitches in the way. I need a mature woman that knows what she wants and can handle a guy like myself. Felicia you tightwork, age ain’t nothing but a number. I think I like you!” Cash said as he looked her in the eyes and placed his hand on her soft thigh.

“Can you turn the fan on it’s um…its getting kind of hot!” She took off her glasses and Cash saw her pretty light brown eyes.

“Leave em on… I like the sophisticated look!” Cash pushed her back and she didn’t resist.

“I don’t do this Cash, it’s the first night! I don’t want you to treat me like the rest!”

“You will never be like the rest baby,” Cash lifted her dress and slid her panties to the side for a taste. “Hmmmmmmmmm…Caaassssshhhh!!!” She yelled out as she stared down at him devour her juices. Felicia hadn't bust a nut in months, so when Cash put his manhood deep inside her she squirted all over him leaking on the couch. He looked down in mid stroke at her juices everywhere. "That's why I got leather!" He went back pounding away at her pussy, if this was the life of a business man he would enjoy it.

$ $ $ $ $ $ $ $ $ $ $ $ $ $ $ $ $

Cash watched from above as Felicia made her way through the crowd and out the door. "Shorty ass fat as shit. You just got done bombin that didn't you?" Rome said as he came in the office and smelled sex in the air.

"You already know bro! Look at this Rome, this jawn poppin. Look at all these people. We made it nigga, this that legit paper. I came from selling candy and pushing dimes on the block now look what a nigga built! I'm bout to come for that Forbes list next." Cash took a sip of his drink and silently thanked God for his fortune and health. This was really going to be a better life. He would be legal for once in his existence. No more drug deals and gun fights. Cash would overcome the obstacle of being a statistic. His destiny was jail or 6 feet under. Now it was looking like island hopping for the summer. The good life.

"We came along way you right bro…I still can't believe it. We been hustling over 10 years my nigga. This shit really reality now. Boss shit!" Rome raised the bottle of champagne in the air as they watched the ladies shake it and the fellas get behind it.

Chapter 20

Always One Up On You

While Cash and Rome were in Atlanta Moose was in Philly on a power trip. He was feeling the power and the powder. W.T.O was in the spot just kicking it and the team was laughing at Moose and how high he was. He was just sitting there dipping so they started joking.

"Ayo bull you can't afford to be dippin like that you already ugly as hell. You look like a husky ass Ethiopian." J-jay joked and the team started cracking up in laughter.

"What's so funny Tank? You think I'm a joke nigga? I did 20 motherfucking years lil nigga! You think you can do that?" Moose stood up aggressively like he wanted to fight.

"Yo bull I'm laughing like everybody else. Don't swell up on me like that Moose I'm far from a bitch!" Tank looked him in his eyes and stood up. He had Moose by weight and height, they both were physical warriors.

"You tellin me what to do nigga? I asked you a fuckin question. You think you can do 20 years nigga? Look at me I'm the boss around this bitch!" Moose quickly pulled out his gun and put it to Tank's stomach.

"You the boss bull, you got it. C'mon we W.T.O put the gun down." Tank had his hands in the air trying to resolve the situation before he was shot.

"Don't get scared now! I wanna know what's so funny? Ain't shit funny with this burner in ya face is it. I never liked ya husky ass anyway! You use to be W.T.O!!!" Moose looked around the room and everyone's face was serious. He put the gun to Tank's head.

"Chill Moose you tripping! That's Tank nigga is you that high?" J-jay said as he watched from across the room, he saw it in Tank's face, he was terrified. Moose lowered the gun and fired a shot in Tank's chest.

"Arrgghhhh what the fuck!!" Tank held his bleeding wound and fell back on the couch.

"Yo bull you fuckin crazy! That's the team nigga! C'mon let's get him to a hospital!" Redz yelled as he came to Tank's aid. Moose just stood there with the smoking gun.

"No need for the spital Redz. He dead!" Everyone paused and looked at Tank who was still alive and fighting.

"Fuck that ! I'm good take me to the hospital please!!! Arrrgghhh! I can make it!" Tank screamed out in pain holding his chest with tears in his eyes and blood seeping through his fingers. Moose snorted a line off the table as Redz helped Tank to his feet.

"He not gonna make it!" BOC BOC BOC!!!"

"Awww shit what the fuck!" J-jay blurted out.

"Daaammmn bull!" Redz said as Tank's body slumped over on the floor bleeding and lifeless.

"I told you he wasn't going to make it." Moose sat down and placed the gun on the table. "He was police y'all! A fuckin rat that nigga was wired!" Moose claimed.

Redz tore Tank's bloody shirt to check for a wire because he didn't believe it.

"Look nigga he ain't got shit but holes in his chest from you! Ain't no fuckin wire bull!" Moose went over to Tank's body and started pulling his pants down.

"What the hell?" W.T.O watched as Moose pulled a wire that was around Tank's testicles and held it in the air. "I told y'all niggas. A fuckin rat!!!"

W.T.O sat there in silence as they saw one of their own laying in a pool of blood. They all were confused at why and how Moose knew. The team was based on loyalty and respect and Tank had violated. He wouldn't be missed.

Chapter 21

Caught Up

Tank was in a rush, he was already late to get to a customer Moose had put him on that wanted some work. He was in his baby momma car because the H2 was getting brakes down on it. His 44 was under the seat just in case it was a problem. He ran a stop sign and saw the blue and red lights behind him. He pulled over and the two officers got out their vehicle to approach.

"These niggas drawin I gotta go!"

"License and registration please." The officer at the driver side window asked. The other officer was at the passenger side with his hand on his gun waiting for Tank to make a sudden move.

"Look bull I ain't got time for this shit. Check the chain nigga, W.T.O, ain't ya check extra husky cuz of us. Back the fuck up and let me go I got shit to do." The officer looked at the chain and then at his partner. He knew that W.T.O was off limits but he was told they would have customized plates. The car Tank was driving didn't.

"That's a nice chain sir but I was told all members would have the license plate. I wouldn't even pull you if I saw it. You just have a chain and anyone can get that. Just step out the car please."

"Did you just hear me nigga. I'm W.T.O and this chain too fuckin icy for anybody to get it. Can you afford it nigga? It cost a two year salary at your job. Just let me go!" Just as he pleaded his case another squad car pulled up to assist. Another two officers stepped up.

"We have a problem fellas?" The other officer said as he and his partner approached.

"Yes the suspect won't cooperate and get out the car."

He looked in the car and saw how huge Tank was and pulled out his night stick.

"Sir I need you to get out of the car before we have to use force. All this can be avoided if you just step out the car."

"Ard ,ard but when y'all get this shit figured out I want badge numbers cuz I got rights and."

Tank was cut short as the officers tackled him to the ground and began beating him with the night sticks to get the cuffs on. They finally got him cuffed after they pepper sprayed him. The cops put him in the back of the cop car and began the search of his vehicle. They found his gun and 3 kilos of cocaine. He kept yelling in the backseat as they pulled off to take him to the station. "I'm W.T.O I'm W.T.O!!!"

$ $ $ $ $ $ $ $ $ $ $ $ $ $ $ $ $

With that amount of drugs and a firearm the Feds got involved. Special Agent Galvin came in the room they had Tank sitting in.

"I know who you are Tank and I know about W.T.O."

Agent Galvin said and slapped a folder down on the table. Tank sat there with his arms crossed and sipping a Sprite the cop gave him. Even in custody his huge presence demanded respect.

"So let me go I told them nut ass cops I was W.T.O! They beat my ass! What the fuck is all this back room police station give him a soda offer him a cigarette shit! Can I leave now and get that work back?" Tank asked looking in Agent Galvin's face so seriously.

"First off I don't give a rat's ass about W.T.O!! This is a lot of coke and a weapon from a convicted Felon.Your going down unless you help me. I'm building a case and when the shit hits the fan you better get yours now. Help me help you so you can see your kids again." Tank sat there quiet, he was confused, who was this and why was he threating him with this time he thought. "What are you saying?"

"Cash, Rome, W.T.O and the shipment I need something solid. If not I'm putting you down as king pin. You just riding around and getting it huh? Bricks and a gun! You just a real gangster. Talk Tank. Let me know those dirty little secrets before I take you off the street for good."

"Nigga get me my lawyer before I get up and slap the shit outta ya Irish ass! I ain't no fuckin rat! Get the fuck out my face!" Tank screamed but he didn't budge Agent Galvin at all. He had seen his type before, harder, bigger and smarter. They all crack...when it all falls down they all crack and he gets his man. His target this time was Cash and W.T.O. He was determined to reel this fish in. He opened his folder and slid a picture of Cash in his Range Rover. "Let's start off slow, who is this?" Tank looked down at the picture then back to Agent Galvin.

"Never seen him before."

"Okay good I thought you might say that. Now look at this picture and then think reeeeeaaal hard with that little brain of yours and if you don't tell me who the fuck is in that first picture yours kids won't see either one forever! Not 10, not 20, that's easy, some of you lil fucks can handle that. Forever!" Tank saw the picture of his child's mother making a drop off for him. He always had her take this guy 3 bricks this guy 5 bricks, and bring back the money and it will never be short. Tank was getting 50 kilos himself a week from the shipment to flip whole sale. When he was somewhere and couldn't get to a customer he would remember his voice clear as day.

"Hold up let me call my baby momma, I'm a call you right back!" This particular picture showed her receiving a bag from Redz it was Tank's cut of the shipment. She was putting it in the trunk. His heart dropped and his palms got sweaty. He didn't even realize it until he heard it escape his lips. "Cash!"

"Good, good, now we're talking the same language." Agent Galvin said with a smile patting Tank on the shoulder with excitement. Tank shook his head what was he to do he couldn't let her go to jail over his shit he thought. "Look if I do this shit I can't see a cell. Niggas gonna get me outta here, they paper stupid. I need immunity me and my baby mom. Put me somewhere in the sticks with my kids. I can't see a cell yo, I can't see a cell!" Tank held his head down in disgust. He never thought he would see the day he would sell his team out.

"Before you start demanding shit I want you wired up! I want you around Cash and Rome talking drugs, talking killings, I want Cash!! Get around him. They rest of them, I don't care they small fries."

"They outta town right now Cash not even in the game. He quit, if I come around him talking some street shit he might shoot me and find the wire. Rome I might can slide up on, he more cool and flashy. Cash done he retired."

"Well you better get me something I can use or kiss ya baby mom and kids goodbye for the last time. I get my man. I will un retire that ass hole and then lock him up. You hear me! Get me something I can use. W.T.O will crumble. Now get the fuck out of here I hate snitches! You big for nothing I just won 500 bucks I bet my partner out there looking in that you would cooperate once I showed you the picture. Thanks!" Tank stood up out the chair and walked toward the door.

"A big guy! Don't forget to see my partner and get wired up before you leave!" Tank listened to him with his back turned and then slammed the door behind him.

$ $ $ $ $ $ $ $ $ $ $ $ $ $ $ $ $

"Ayo whassup with you?" Moose asked Tank who was sitting on the couch in a daze. Moose had Juicy on his lap and a pile of coke by his side on a small mirror about 28grams. They were in the spot waiting for Fat Mike to drop his cut of the week's take from Lansdowne Ave.

"Same shit different day. I'm tired as shit!" Tank didn't even look him in the eyes he was still shocked at what was going on. He was actually wired with it around his balls. He told them it couldn't be on his chest that would really have him nervous.

"I know what will wake you up. Ayo Juicy go suck dat nigga dick loosen him up he need some pussy!" Juicy stood up with a seductive look on her face and made her way toward Tank. He began to sweat as she neared. This was not happening. He had to play it cool so he pulled it together the best he could. "Naw bull I'm good. I just buss my baby momma ass! She drained me that bitch don't let me leave the house without dropping down getting every drop. This money make her love dis big ass nigga!" Tank laughed.

"Hold up not Tank ya big ugly ass ain't turning down no pussy what's wrong nigga, who died? Ya bitch cheating?"

"Naw nigga my bitch faithful, I'm cool chill! What the fuck Moose can a nigga have his days. I'm chilling my nigga I don't want no head from this bitch! I just wanna go home take a good shit and go to bed. That's how I'm feeling." Tank snapped.

"My bad Mr. Emotional, well back to business you handle that?"

"What?" Tank asked totally unaware of what he was talking about.

"You ain't that fucked up nigga, that work you handle that?"

"The coke yeah I sold it Moose! This me Tank nigga I get rid of it."

"So where my money you ain't bring me the bread."

"Yeah it's at my bitch crib." Tank forgot the Feds took the drugs and his gun. When they told him leave he wired up and came straight to Thompson to the spot. "Yeah I told her to count it when I hollered at ya peoples. I just went there and gave them the coke. I got the money and dropped it off to her. Then I came straight here I thought you said we had a meeting."

"Why the fuck ya bitch counting my money. Ayo go get my fuckin bread Tank you on some real super stupid shit right now I don't know whassup with you. She might short my shit and blame it on my peoples, and it's ya bitch tuckin cuz you ain't count it when you seen em. You drawin bull!"

"I got you, I be back bull!" Tank got up and left out thinking how this had to come out of his stash. Moose shook his head as Tank left.

"Big dumb ass nigga. Get my chicken you got ya bitch countin my shit. You hear that nigga Juicy? C'mere girl eat that dick up." Moose told Juicy while grabbing his crotch. He felt his phone vibrate.

"Ayo Moose is Tank cool?"

"Who the fuck is this?" He said anxious to know what happened that fast when Tank just left.

"This Frog, I was in traffic when I saw the Police put him in the back of the car earlier. They sprayed him and everything bull, fucked him up. He was tellin em he W.T.O they wasn't listening." Moose was confused Tank didn't say anything about getting locked up. He was acting strange and looked a little roughed up.

"He got locked up today? You sure nigga?"

"Earlier bro I was in traffic when they cuffed him and sprayed his eyes with the pepper jawn! Real rap! I'm just seeing if he coo, that's why I called you!"

"True, yeah he cool, he cool. Ayo good look I'm out bull!" Moose hung up and it he couldn't believe it. Then he called his peoples that Tank was suppose to serve.

"Yo bull, my man see you today? So he never showed up? Damn bro that's crazy I think this bitch ass nigga switch sides! Yeah, I see you Friday I'm a look out and toss you one, my bad!" Moose hung up and it all made sense.

$ $ $ $ $ $ $ $ $ $ $ $ $ $ $ $ $

"What up nigga?" Redz asked Tank as he came in the spot with the bag of money took from his safe at the house. He sat on the couch and took the cash out. It was 60 grand Moose was selling them for 20 apiece and told Tank just to go handle that for him.

"Same shit you know where Moose at?"

"Upstairs. Ayo tell this nigga J-jay I fucked the bitch Shernev he think I gotta lie about a chick from around the way. He hit years ago I just hit! The pussy better now and he mad!" Redz laughed and J-jay waited for Tank to respond.

"Yeeeah he did J he pulled up in that Aston on her she thought it was a space ship. We was in that jawn blowin some Cali shit, that shit was some bomb. I remember I got out, and then she got in and they was out!"

Moose came downstairs as everyone was laughing and saw Tank and the bag of money on the table. He was really playing the role like he saw his peoples.

"Yo Moose I got that paper from that coke I sold for you!" Redz and J-jay were still conversing about females and Moose was observing. He knew Tank was a rat because nobody talks like that, his peoples never got served and he had the money on the table. It wasn't looking good for Tank Moose thought.

"True dat. He still got them pretty ass pit bulls runnin around the spot? I told him he gonna make me shoot one of them bitches!" Moose asked waiting for Tank to lie.

"Yeah he had them bitches out. They mean as hell I said I wanna check if I get bit." Tank looked him in the eyes with a straight face.

"So here go your money for those 3 bricks I sold for you!"

"Ayo stop talking like that bro I know what it is.Damn Tank you working with the boys or something?" The room got quiet and everyone looked at Tank. "HA HA HA HA HA!!" They all burst out in laughter but Moose wasn't really laughing as hard as they were.

"You funny nigga stop playing. I be back I gotta take my girl somewhere so hit me later." Tank got up and walked toward the door.

"Ayo Tank come back like 12, we chilling the whole team W.T.O baby!" Moose said.

"W.T.O all day!" Tank responded with authority. He nodded and was out the door. He drove straight to meet up with Agent Galvin that had to be enough he couldn't do anymore.

"I got you Moose that should be good enough!" Tank said pulling up on Kelly Drive where they planned to meet. "I heard it I heard it. But Tank I want Cash. Get him to talk about Cash. You doing good for your first day, I like that."

"I'm going back at 12." Tank told him ready to do whatever to save his self regardless of who he had to cross. "

You will never see a jail cell if you continue on this path. I keep my word. I will send 2 agents in a van with you. They will park down the block and listen in the whole time to back you up." Agent Galvin informed him.

"Whoa its look outs from 49th to 52nd they gotta park further away. That odd ass van too suspicious." Tank told him because he knew them lookouts were on point. Cash paid them and everybody else more than well. That built loyalty and they really appreciated playing their position on the team. Being apart of W.T.O was like a hood honor. They all were getting money.

"I got your back. You my Kobe right now. Go get me another championship!" Agent Galvin shook his hand and Tank got back in his car and headed home.

$ $ $ $ $ $ $ $ $ $ $ $ $ $ $ $ $ $

"Can I get some money to go shopping?" Tank's girl said as soon as he stepped foot in the door.

"Damn girl let me get in the house first! Can I take a shit? Maybe something to eat, all you want is some fucking money! You don't give a fuck about me!" His bottled up frustration erupted and he snapped on her.

"You just want ya dick sucked all day that shit cost! Don't take ya period out on me cuz you had a bad day in them streets. Fuck dat Tank fuck you!"

"My bad you right, you ain't got nothing to do with what's going on baby. I'm sorry, can you just hold ya big teddy bear I need it."

"Yeah, after I go shopping, my girls waiting on me babe. When I get back I got you and I'm a suck it how you like cuz you my big teddy bear." Tank pulled out his bank roll and gave her $2500 to pick up a few things.

"You better get me something too! The new Jordan's out." She kissed his forehead and left out the house. Tank sat on the couch and flipped through the channels it was 11:30pm and his girl hadn't got back yet. He got up and hopped in his Chevy Caprice on 24's all black with the loud pipes. When he got to the spot he saw Moose feeding his nose as usual and the rest of the team just joking around. Tank was stressing and he needed to relax and forget he was working with the federal government.

"Let me get a hit of that shit you be going in on the coke." Moose just glared his way, just hearing him talk made his skin crawl. He hated rats and Moose figured rats should get exterminated.

$ $ $ $ $ $ $ $ $ $ $ $ $ $ $ $ $

Around the corner from Thompson Street in a Peco Energy van the federal Agents listened in on Tank and the W.T.O organization.

"Shit I hope he don't sniff a lot of that shit his balls will start sweating and fuck the wire up!" Agent Miles said as he heard Tank say he wanted to get some coke.

"That really will mess it up a little sweat?" Agent Stockton said eating a cheese steak. He hated the stake out part of his job. He just wanted to crack heads and close the case and let these drug dealers kill their self.

"If he sniffs too much it will distort the wire. This is a big case we can't blow this!"

$ $ $ $ $ $ $ $ $ $ $ $ $ $ $ $ $

"Y'all niggas some coke heads I'm a stick to this Haze." Redz told Moose and Tank who were feeding their nose. Tank took two lines back to back and was done. His eyes watered and he was just laughing as the team began to crack jokes.

"You a funny looking motherfucka, I bet you had an ugly ass mug shot!" J-jay told Moose and everyone was just laughing hard.

"Ayo Moose I know you ain't gonna let J grind you up like dat?" Redz said.

"You is a funny looking dude tho Moose," Tank added as he pointed and burst out laughing. Moose looked at Tank with fire in his eyes. He wanted to smack Tank head off his shoulders. "What's so funny Tank? You think I'm a joke lil nigga? I did twenty motherfucking years! You think you can do that?"

$ $ $ $ $ $ $ $ $ $ $ $ $ $ $ $ $ $

"Fuck we lost the signal! He sniffing all that shit his balls probably soaking wet!" Agent Miles said. "So what do we do now?" They sat back and hoped they could get the signal back, for right now it was all static. After a few minutes they heard a gunshot rang out and it sounded close.

"Fuck you think that was our guy?" Agent miles said and more shots rang out close by.

"That's our ass if it was him. Galvin's going to shit a brick!" Agent Baylor stated.

$ $ $ $ $ $ $ $ $ $ $ $ $ $ $ $ $

The W.T.O team sat in the house in silence as they looked at Tank's body wrapped in sheets. "Fuck waiting I'm not sitting in this bitch with no dead body, we good we can take my wheel. Lets drop his big ass off bull!" J-jay blurted out. Moose told them to drop him off at Fairmount Park so Redz and J-jay tossed Tank's body in the trunk and they were off.

When they finally got to Fairmount Park it was almost 5 in the morning. Redz got the shovels out the back and they began to dig. J-jay was just shocked at what they were doing, burying one of their own. He couldn't believe Tank. J-jay loved this life, he could do anything he wanted. His life was worth living because of W.T.O. They built an empire that blessed them with wealth he never imagined. Respect where it mattered to him, in the streets. He would never work a 9 to 5 again in his life and Cash gave them a way out. $300,000 was easy money to walk away from it all, but they all stuck to the G Code.

"Ayo Redz I can't believe Tank was a snitch…I would never take that route bro." J-jay said as they took Tank's body from the trunk and tossed him in the hole.

"We chose this shit and Cash gave us all a chance to get out this shit. But he was thinking like we all were. That 300 sounded good but it's the lifestyle we not tryna give up for real. Shit hurt a little because he W.T.O, we all got our chains together. Remember how they was dickeattin when we first started?" J-jay found his self going down memory lane. Redz stopped throwing dirt on the body and slammed the shovel in the grass. "This clown ass nigga was a rat! He deserve to be right where he at. Real shit! I ain't got no remorse for this bitch ass nigga." Redz spit on the dirt that Tank was buried under. "He ain't W.T.O he pussy!" Redz yelled down in the hole. Tank was his closet homie in the squad after Rome introduced him. He was hurt more than J-jay would ever know.

$ $ $ $ $ $ $ $ $ $ $ $ $ $ $ $ $ $ $ $

The next morning was gloomy and the dark clouds and light rain assured it was a bad day. Special Agent Galvin was downtown at the federal building infuriated in the meeting he held. When Tank didn't show up for their appointment and then he heard the wire was distorted his day turned to shit. He looked around the room and it was quiet. He glared at Agent Baylor, then Agent miles.

"We suppose to be the FBI not the local PPD. The drug dealers are laughing at us, it's okay to sell drugs. It's okay to kill people! I got a missing informant and a wire that doesn't give us dick! I will not lose you hear me? I have been doing this for 18 years and I always get my man. Say hello to my plan B ladies and gentlemen." Everyone watched the door open and a beautiful thick African American woman with light brown eyes came in with a grey pin striped business suit. She was thin in the waist and thick where every man wanted. The men in the room mouths slowly opened in awe. Her full pink lips and brown skin was smooth.

"Everyone this is undercover Agent Robin Jones. She did some good work with us down in New York on that guy Malik Sonz. He was pushing heroin from New York to Philaelphia distributing through the Kensington area in North Philly. Agent Jones was a major part to that bust she became his girlfriend and he involved her in his daily drug activity. Her testimony was the key to his conviction."

Agent Robin Jones looked around at her co-workers as they admired her credentials and Agent Galvin continued.

"I am confident that Agent Jones will get us some solid evidence and we can take something real to the grand jury. I told you people I get my man and whatever it takes to do that I will." Agent Galvin was so serious. He put his life into his work. He was on his forth marriage and at 56 all he enjoyed was locking up his target. That caused long nights that tore every relationship he had in his life to pieces.

Chapter 22

The Love & Set Up

W.T.O was posted outside on Thompson Street. Moose and J-jay sat on the steps while Redz leaned against the Benz.

"Ayo who these bitches coming up the block? She tight work?!" Redz blurted out as he inhaled the smoke from the Dutch. Everyone looked but no one recognized them. Moose was the first to get up when they got close enough.

"I haven't seen you before you a new face. Can a man show you how a goddess such as yourself is suppose to be treated? What is your name?" Agent Jones was in character that's what she liked to call it when undercover. There was a room for rent on 50th street so Agent Galvin sent her in. The location was perfect because it was right around the corner from Thompson Street. She smiled and even though Moose was older, jail preserved him. His body was in tip top shape. She eyed his husky arms then back at him and spoke.

"Tiffany and I just moved around here I live on 50th street."

"Oh you got that jawn where they renting rooms. Yo where ya man you can't be living in no room baby?" Redz and J-jay were talking to her roommate and had her laughing so he had Tiffany's full attention.

"I take care of myself and I do what I can with my lil dollars. That's all I can afford." Moose felt bad for her because she was too fine to be not taken care of. He was ready to put a ring on it at first sight. She licked her lips and he eyed those juicy pink lips as she moistened them with her tongue slowly.

"Why you looking at me like dat?"

"No bullshit I will suck a fart out ya butt!" She smiled and laughed at his humor.

"Shhhit you laughing I'm dead serious bend over!" She laughed even harder and punched his arm playfully.

"Shut up you stupid! I don't even know ya name you suck farts out of all the girls butts around here?"

"I'm Musa but everybody call me Moose."

"Well I will call you Musa because I'm not everyone." She said and they joined in on all the laughter and giggles Redz and J-jay was giving her room mate.

"Ayo Tiffany these niggas too funny,You boo loving already I told you to come out that room. She been here for two weeks and all she do is be in that room. I told her she need to get some air. Now look she might got one." Natalie was a petite light skin girl with a lot of sass. She didn't take no shit and her pretty hazel eyes and bright smile lured the guys in. When the two black Bentleys pulled up the conversation stopped.

"Look at these niggas! That's how y'all do huh. Back to back Bents on these niggas?"J-Jay said as Rome and Cash hopped out on them. They drove back to Philly doing 100 plus all the way. The luxury cars floated on the interstate and now the duo was back in the city checking on the team.

"We back in the city what's good?" Cash said as he shook hands with his boys. Agent Jones had hit the jackpot and was now around Cash and Rome, her main targets. She looked Cash up and down. He was in some crisp True Religion jeans, some construction Timberlands and a white polo v neck t-shirt with his West Philly chain swinging. He looked at her and then at Moose. Rome was bold he looked at Natalie and licked his lips, he loved a petite female.

"Who these bitches Moose? Y'all got couple day on the block whassup?" Rome said and J-jay and Redz started laughing. Natalie wasn't feeling being called a bitch. She walked up on Rome pointing her finger in his face. "Nigga you don't know me watch who you call a bitch for real!" She sincerely stated with authority.

"Bitch if you don't get the fuck out my face. Do you even know me? Back the fuck up before I slap the shit out you shorty!"

"I said, I ain't no bitch nigga!" She smacked Rome across the face. Everyone just looked shocked at what just happened. Rome held his face which had turned red. Rome grabbed her face with one hand.

"Bitch is you fuckin crazy? Are you?" He shook her face while he clutched it with one hand. "Bitch I could kill you!"

"Do it nigga!" She mumbled behind his hand. Rome couldn't believe how hard she was. He looked in her eyes and then looked at her full lips that seemed so soft. His dick got hard and he went in for the kiss. She had really turned him on. She was bold and he liked that.

"Nigga you don't know me! Don't be kissing me like dat!" She yelled as he gripped her up and went in for another one. This kiss was with tongue, wet and sloppy. They both just stood there tonguing each other down. The attraction was mutual.

"Damn baby no one ever put they hands on me and got away with it. What's ya name I like you, you got a man?" Rome asked the pretty eyed tough girl that stood in front of him.

"Yeah I do and I'm very happy!" She stated but Rome could tell she was missing something in her life and her response wasn't convincing at all. Rome gave her a piece of paper with his number on it.

"Make sure you call me if bull not playing his part. I'm on ya top lil butt!" She smiled and tucked the number in her back pocket.

"My butt ain't little nigga, I got a donk!" She laughed and poked it out.

Cash had come out the spot with 2 duffel bags. He gave one to Rome and tossed the other in the trunk of the Bentley.

"Y'all niggas be easy we outta here!" Cash looked at the girl with Moose one last time and then hopped in his car and peeled off with Rome following.

"Who were they Musa?" Tiffany asked.

"That's the team W.T.O. Cash my lil cousin and Rome his right hand man."

"What is W.T.O?" Natalie blurted out.

"You ain't never heard of us? C'mon don't fraud you heard of W.T.O!" J-jay added as he pulled on the Dutch and blew smoke from his nose and mouth.

"Not me!" Natale said.

"I think I did hear of y'all. This girl in the hair salon was like W.T.O this, Cash that, Rome this, just telling all y'all business. She like they tryna get everybody in West Philly rich. They on some black Mob shit." Tiffany lied telling her story. She got her information from the federal government. Moose looked at her and smiled.

"That's some of it, c'mon let's go!" Moose stuck his hand out for her to grab.

"What about my roommate?"

"She just smacked a cold killer she good!" Tiffany looked back at Natalie and she told her to have fun and go. Moose and Tiffany got in his 745 and drove off leaving Redz, J, and Natalie still on the steps smoking.

"So whassup Nat a nigga tryna bomb, like I'm a real nigga! Whassup wit the whassup?" Natalie looked at Redz with an irritated look on her face. "Damn that's how y'all do on Thompson Street huh, just tag team bitches? Ya man just came at me now you on it!" She stood up and passed the Dutch to J-jay.

"I'm cool I don't want none of y'all dicks. I got a man, bye boy! Thanks for the Haze." She turned and made her way down the block.

"Damn nigga you always scare the pussy away. You drawed, let em breath nigga!" J-jay said.

"Man fuck dat bitch she skinny anyway, I like big country ghetto booties. Fuck dat bitch!" Redz said and checked his phone for who he was about to hit up for a quickie.

$ $ $ $ $ $ $ $ $ $ $ $ $ $ $ $ $

When Natalie walked to her house she saw her boyfriend Kev outside her home. She walked up with a smile. “Hey boo I was just talking about you.”

“Bitch I seen you on the steps talking to them niggas being all fuckin joe. Get the fuck in this house so I don’t make a scene.” Natalies’s heart raced, she was scared and tired of the abuse. Every time he didn’t like something, or had a bad day he would slap her around and beat her up like a man. She wanted to leave so bad but was afraid he might try to do more than beat her up. She walked up and put her key in the door and walked in with him closely behind. “Baby I just------

He smacked her to the floor busting her lip. “Bitch you up there suckin dick?!” He kicked her in the ribs hard.

“Ahhhhhhhh Kev stop!! I didn’t do nothing I swear baby, please stoooop!” She cried out and tried to block the swings that came next.

“You cheating on me! Bitch you tryna play me for these nut ass niggas around here? I will kill you! Keep playing!!” He kicked her again even harder.

“Take ya ass upstairs and clean up! You look like somebody just beat ya ass!” Natalie slowly got to her feet blocking her face and ran upstairs. She cried when she saw her face in the mirror of the bathroom. She hated her life. This was not a healthy relationship. He yelled from downstairs.

“You better be pretty when I come up there. I want some pussy so you better look like Beyonce when I get up that bitch.” He screamed and she reached in her pocket for Rome’s number. Maybe this was her way out she thought. Maybe Rome was different and could give her what she needed. She was done with Kev this time. He never was about nothing and if she faked another orgasm she would die. He forced his way on her everyday and for 7 years nothing changed, it just got worst.

"Hello," she cried.

Rome looked at the number and didn't recognize it or the voice.

"Who is this?"

"It's me Natalie…can you come get me? Please my dude beat my ass and im done. I hate him! Please Rome!" She just started crying I the phone.

"Chill chill I will be there. Look I know chicks that get fucked up and still come back. If I come get you, that situation over, you hear me?"

"Hurry I'm done with this shit my address 5023 n 50th street."

"I just got back down this way. Be there in a minute."

"Yo bitch I need my dick sucked hurry up and get ya ass down here!" Kev yelled as he sat on the couch with his hands in his pants. He heard a banging at the door.

"Who the fuck is it?" He screamed and stood to his feet to see who was banging on the door. He swung the door open and the first thing he saw was the W.T.O chain around Rome's neck.

"What the fuck you want nigga?"

"I came to get Natalie is she ready?" Rome said calmly.

"Nigga you come over my crib and ask for my bitch is you crazy? I don't care about no fucking WTO, fuck y'all!! I'm a North Philly rider you clown ass nigga."

Rome looked Rico in the eyes and saw he was timid, doing time and being in the street gave him the ability to read people. He choked him up and dragged him out of the house. Kev began to turn blue as Rome squeezed his neck tighter and tighter. Natalie watched from the door way as Rome was choking the life out of her longtime lover.

"Watch ya fuckin mouth nigga and keep ya hands off females. Real talk nigga I will kill you if ever come around here again." Rome saw him fading out so he loosened his grip just a little.

"Wake up nigga! You hear me? You call her or get somebody else to call her your dead. This Rome girl now nigga! Try me!" Rome let his neck go as he blacked out. He looked up at Natalie and told her to get in the car.

"Naw fuck him up Rome he getting off too easy. Fuck dat nigga up!" She said as she got in the car and slammed the door. Rome looked at her and laughed.

"She crazy!" Kev started to come to and Rome stood over him. Rome punched him in the face with 5 stiff jabs as he held him by the shirt with his other hand.

"You like beatin bitches like they niggas huh! You that type of nigga?" Rome punches were like slashes across Kev's face and his skin split as each blow connected and blood gushed out.

"Get up nigga!" Rome got husky with him and pulled his slumped body from the ground and swung his head into a car windshield. Glass shattered as he went head first through the driver window.

"Clean ya pretty ass up! Your bleeding everywhere." Rome chuckled and got in the car with his new girl and got out of there.

$ $ $ $ $ $ $ $ $ $ $ $ $ $ $ $ $

"So Musa I know you sell drugs. But is there something else you want to do with your life?" Tiffany asked as they walked through the Philadelphia Zoo. It surprised her when he brought her to the Zoo but she thought it was sweet. Moose smile before he answered her.

"Listen I did 20 years in prison I just came home. I don't know shit but what I do. Look all that time I did and that's all I did, do time. I was suppose to get a trade, my G.E.D, something. I smoked, drank, worked out and worked out some more for twenty years. I don't have time to bullshit you. Your beautiful you should let me love you!"

"Awww Musa that was sweet! Let's just take it slow and see what happens. I've been hurt so many times. I just want to find Mr. right not Mr. right now." She held his hand and they walked through the Zoo getting to know each other.

On the ride back to the neighborhood Tiffany turned the radio down. She needed info and the Zoo trip was cool but it wasn't beneficial to her case.

"Baby don't drop me off I thought I was with you all day today!" She said sadly.

"I got business later but I can come get you later."

"That's not all dayyyyy, I wanna be with you don't leave me already!" Moose took a deep breath he didn't want to bring her while he did his business, but it was felt great that she wanted to be around him.

"Fuck it I just gotta holla at my lil cuz that's it. I guess you can roll with me." He placed his hand on her thigh and they headed toward Cash's house.

They pulled up in front of Cash's house and the Range Rover and the Cadillac truck were in the driveway, the CTS and X5 was parked on the street with the Bentley. Tiffany looked around and the neighborhood was nice. She pulled out her cell phone and snuck a picture of the front of his house. Moose led the way as they walked in. Cash was on the couch smoking a Dutch. When Cash saw Moose he got up and gave him a handshake. "Ayo Moose I been calling Tank all fuckin day whassup wit em?"

"Maaannnn that nigga was a rat cuz I forgot to tell you. I bodied his bitch ass!" Moose said proudly as Tiffany stood behind him. Cash looked at her and then Moose.

"You wildin cuz. Pretty girl can you excuse us the remote on the table help yourself." Cash took Moose to the den.

"Damn bull you talkin reckless in front of shorty. How long you knew this bitch you bringing her to my crib and shit?"

"She cool cuz I been fuckin with her for a while now." Moose lied. He knew he was out of line for bringing her here but he didn't want to lose his chance with her. His mind was made up, Tiffany was going to be his woman.

"How the fuck you know Tank was a rat? You still sniffin that coke?" Cash snapped.

"I found the wire on him cuz and yeah I'm still doing it but I slowed down since we talked about it." Cash couldn't believe Moose found a wire on Tank. He was a gangster. Tank never showed ways of a snitch, if he did Cash would have never put him in position. He was glad Moose took care of it and patted him on the back.

“Good job tho cuz. I’m glad you were on point about that. Y’all take care of the body?”

“We good cuz…we good!”

Chapter 23

Me and My Girlfriend

It had been six months since Tiffany and Moose met, they had finally made it official last month to be a couple. Moose had stopped sniffing coke and stuck to the weed. He bought a house in Northeast Philly and Tiffany moved in with him. She told him she had an office job downtown as a secretary. Moose was really feeling his girl and he wasn't even cheating.

On the other hand Rome was taking Natalie serious but he still had sex with every female that got his dick hard. He and Natalie made it official after the first month, she still lived in the hood but Rome paid the rent and bought her a car. Everything was good with WTO. Cash was back and forth to Atlanta and working on his next club. He was still seeing Felicia every time he was in Atlanta. Moose finally got the whole South West on smash and was doing big numbers on the crack side. Redz had a little heroin in South Philly doing numbers and W.T.O was clocking major paper. Now in West and South West Philly 100% of the crack came from Cash. W.T.O had those areas on lock, and Moose was trying for North. He wanted the city in his hand.

Dallas and Cash, Moose and Tiffany, and Redz being the fifth wheel, were at a pizza place in South Philly. Everybody was relaxing having a good time getting to know each other. Agent Jones was playing her part, but slowly she was beginning to catch feelings for Moose. She felt his genuine love and saw the drastic change he made for her.

"So Tiff, what school did you go to in Houston?" Dallas asked.

"I was home schooled until I went to college," She replied.

"Damn you must have some rich parents to get home schooled for so long," Redz said.

"Come on, I wouldn't say rich, but they had a good income."

"I have to use the ladies room, I'll be back," Dallas said as she got up from the table with her short black Gucci skirt and Gucci blouse to match. Dallas went to the bathroom and Cash was right on her heels. When Dallas went to the sink Cash knocked on the door and came in.

"What you doing Cash this is the ladies room."

"I'm doing you," Cash said as he pulled his pants down and picked Dallas up on the sink.

"You better stop before someone comes in Cash."

"Fuck it baby, I need it now you look too sexy in that dress," Cash pulled down Dallas's thong and slid his manhood in her vagina.

"Damn Cash that shit feels so good, Oh Cash, Oh Cash," she screamed as she wrapped her legs around his waist.

"Don't fucking move, everyone put their money on the table. Empty the register asshole before I blast your ass." The young gunman said as he pointed the shotgun at his face. The man at the register gave him all the money in the cash register.

"Alright, everyone empty your pockets and take off your jewelry!!"

"Shit I just got this damn Jacob," Redz said. Everyone began to empty their pockets and purses.

"Baby don't empty shit," Moose told Tiffany.

"Ayo homie don't do this," Moose said as he stood up.

"Oh you a boss huh, take them chains off! I don't want to hear that shit," the young man said as he pointed the shotgun at Moose.

"Look, I got ten grand in my pocket, just take it and leave, all these people work hard for they money. It will take you a hundred pizza places to get ten grand, so take this and leave." Moose took the two bank rolls out of his pockets and showed the gunman. "Fuck that, I want everything and what's in ya they pocket. I see that watch blinging from over here. I know that's fifty grand by itself, so give it all up."

$ $ $ $ $ $ $ $ $ $ $ $ $ $ $ $ $

"I'm about to cum, Oh shit Cash I'm cummin!!!!" Cash yelled. Dallas's body was trembling as she came with Cash's last thrust. Every stroke was hitting her spot and she couldn't believe how wet she was.

"Please Cash fuck me don't stop keep going!!!" Cash couldn't hold it, he exploded inside of Dallas.

"Damn baby, it's been a minute since I hit that, you been playin since you got that job." Cash pulled up his pants and put her thong in his pocket.

"I know, but I've been tired and really needing to study. I'm a get back on track, I promise. You know I love that dick, now give me my thong."

“I’m a keep these to remember you when you at work. You know I love the smell of ya pussy.” Cash heard screams coming from the restaurant.

“What the fuck?” he peeked out of the bathroom and saw the young guy with the shot gun.

“Get the fuck outta here, this nigga robbing everybody.”

“What? Let me see.” Dallas said hype ready to be nosey.

“Hell no stay here, I’ll be back,” Cash pulled out his 45 and walked out of the restroom. The robber was talking shit to Redz with the shot gun in his face.

“You think you getting money, give me that watch nigga. Y’all them W.T.O niggas, I heard of y’all. A bitch, come up off that that money too, I don’t discriminate.” Cash slowly crept behind him and put the gun to his head. The kid never saw it coming.

“Drop the shotgun pussy! C’mon youngbull before I make a cheese pizza with extra brains.” Cash said and he meant every word. The robber dropped the shotgun he knew how W.T.O got down so he said a silent prayer.

“Alright man chill I don’t got no problems, real rap. Damn just let me live, please, please don’t kill me.” Cash hit him in the back of the head with the gun dropping him to his knees. He looked at the young youth and saw a child. He held the gun to his face as he watched the tears fall from the stick up boy.

“Get the fuck outta here,” Cash kicked him and he ran out of the pizza place holding the back of his head screaming thank God.

Everyone in the pizza shop started clapping. Cash smiled and tucked his gun. “Chill, chill, I was just helping because I had the drop.” Dallas came out clapping and jumped in his arms.

“I love you Cash, that made me so wet, let’s go home.”

“I’ll holla at y’all we out, she ain’t been giving up no pussy in a minute.”

“Shut up Cash,” Dallas gave him a soft punch on the arm. They left and got in Cash’s Range Rover.

$ $ $ $ $ $ $ $ $ $ $ $ $ $ $ $ $ $

“Come on Moose, drop me off at one of my hoes crib,” Redz said. The three got up from the table and got in Moose car to drop Redz off. He listened from the front seat as Redz set up his date. Moose was proud of his self he was done with that life. All he needed was Tiffany.

“Ayo Meeka, I’m on my way, cool, yeah I got the condoms girl, about thirty minutes.”

(Click)

“Ayo Moose, drop me off in North Philly, I got this freak jawn on 19th and Allegheny."

“Come on, you know you need ya own car, cuz I ain’t picking you up later. Me and Tiffany about to make love.” Moose stated with a slight smirk.

“Nigga please, she ain’t give you no pussy yet?” Redz said from the back seat.

“Shut up Redz, he still my baby,” Tiffany said as she rubbed Moose’s leg.

"I don't like drivin my shit in North, them niggas might try me. You can't ball too hard on niggas in they own hood fucking they bitches. I just don't feel like blasting, I wanna just fuck shorty and bounce." Redz phone vibrated and he saw a text from another groupie wanting to see him. He ignored it his mind was set on Meeka. He loved her dick suck.

"You need a hoopty!" Moose suggested.

"Redz don't do hoops no more, I'm W.T.O my nigga," They drove toward North and Moose blasted some EPMD.

"You killing me with this old shit, put that Beans in or some Young Jeezy," Redz yelled.

"Nigga, this is real hip hop fuck Jay, Jeezy, and whoeva else. These cats started that shit. Y'all young niggas don't know shit, in the 80's when hip hop first started I was in my prime." Moose loved his oldschool hip hop music it took him down memory lane, to times before he went to jail.

"Turn right and it's the third house from the corner." Moose pulled up in front of the house and beeped the horn.

"You got ya burner?" Moose asked.

"Come on nigga, you know I'm packing the 44!" Redz showed the gun in his waist band.

"I'll holla at y'all, and Moose come get me at 8:30.Real shit dog. I'm in and out like a robbery with this bitch."

"Nigga, I told you I can't, you better call Rome."

"I can't, cause unlike you, Rome is getting some pussy," Redz joked.

“Well call a cab, I got shit to do.”

“That’s fucked up Moose, but its cool you can be like that.”Redz got out and saw Meeka in her bra and panties at the door. He was about to demolish that pussy. He looked at her flat stomach and those hips. She was his favorite of many little sex buddies.

“See that Moose, I’ll be hitting that while you’ll be cuddling with your girl.” Redz shut the door to the 745 and walked toward the steps. Moose rolled down the window.

“Ayo, you gonna wear them chains and shit?” Moose yelled.

“Hell yeah, I bought them I’m wearing them. These niggas better not try shit!” Redz lifted his shirt up. “Remember nigga?” He walked in the house and Moose pulled off and called Jay-J.

“Ayo Jay-J, come get Redz at 8:30, he over the bitch Meeka crib that we ran the train on when I got out. Remember 8:30 don’t be late.” (Click)

“Y’all ran a what?” Tiffany snapped.

“That’s the past baby, you know that. Besides, I’m tired of waiting to hit that, I should make a U-turn and get some Meeka.” Moose joked.

“What nigga don’t think I can’t get hood.”

“Baby chill, you don’t even sound hood.”

$ $ $ $ $ $ $ $ $ $ $ $ $ $ $ $ $

The hours passed and Jay-J was heading to North in his new 2006 Navigator on 24's. Redz was done with Meeka and it was 8:26. He hit her about four times and got his dick sucked for about an hour straight.

"Aye shorty, I'm a wait outside for my man and blow dis port. Bring ya big ass out here!" Redz and Meeka sat on the steps and waited for Jay-J. The local hustlers in the hood were on the corner playing dice. A young guy passed and looked at Redz.

"What's good Tameeka?" the young guy said.

"Hey T, I'll be ready to braid ya hair later tonight."

"Cool, what's good homeboy, I see you blinging." The young kid said to Redz with a slick smirk.

"Yeah, that's what getting money do to you." Redz responded and adjusted his huge gun in his waist band.The young guy kept walking and joined the rest of the hustlers at the corner.

"Dude think he gangstaor something? I should air that whole fuckin corner out!" Redz told Meeka. She didn't want any drama where she rested her head. She knew how Redz got down and heard the many stories of W.T.O.

"Chill Redz don't do nothing crazy! I live here don't draw on my house."

"Chill bitch ain't nobody about to draw on ya crib these niggas just think they goons out here so much until you lay they nut ass!" Redz dialed J to see where he was at before shots fired. "Yo bull where you at?"

“Like 5 minutes away why whassup?”

“Just hurry up before I draw out here. Some lil dusty ass lil nigga said some flea shit. Get here my nigga!”

“On my way bull.” Just as Redz hung up the phone he saw the young kid and three other dudes coming his way. Redz knew something was about to pop off.

“Meeka sit between my legs. I got something for these younens.” She stood up and positioned herself between his legs on the steps. Redz pulled out the 44 and held it behind her back.

“Please Redz don’t do nothing stupid.” Meeka pleaded as the little gangsters were at the bottom of the steps staring at him mean mugging.

“Yo bull you from around here?” The kid said with his homies backing him up.

“I’m from West! What’s this, 21 questions? Fuck outta here youngbull y’all got the wrong one!” The kid wasn’t older than 18 his friends were all 19 and 20. He looked at his squad and they pulled out their guns. Redz shook his head at them. Young guys were always quick to shoot somebody over nothing these days.

“Come up off them chains nigga and that watch! Meeka get out the way!”

“This the second time today someone tried to take my watch. Real shit you gonna need a fuckin army to get this off my wrist!” Redz came over Meeka’s shoulder with his .44 and the young crew froze.

“C’mon we can start squeezin! Real shit I’m a take 3 of y’all with me. The one I leave alive just gonna tell the story of the crazy ass nigga from West that aired shit!” They all just aimed their guns in silence. J-jay turned the corner and saw Redz was in trouble. He pulled the SK from the backseat and rolled his passenger window down as he rolled up on them.

“We got problems?” J yelled and the young thugs eyes grew wide and one ran off the break leaving his team.

“Naw we cool!” The one that started it all blurted out seeing the heavy machine gun aimed in their direction.

“So drop the guns then.” J ordered ready to let every bullet leave the clip on them. They dropped the guns and Redz came down the steps with his gun in hand.

“I told y’all lil niggas keep it pushin!” Redz quickly punched two of them in the face knocking them to the ground. He stepped up on the final kid and hit him with a hard gut shot he bent over gasping for air and coughing.

“Gimmie ya wrist nigga!” The kid put his arm up and Redz took his watch off and put in on his wrist. He hit him across the face with the gun. “ARRGGHHH!”

“You wanna die over a watch nigga? This shit was worth ya life? Was it lil nigga?” Redz screamed as he held the gun to the kid’s nose as his friend’s watched from the concrete. “Noooo, I swear I don’t I was drawin!” He cried out and Redz saw the puddle of piss he was in.

“I really should kill you lil niggas. Gimmie my fuckin watch!” The kid quickly took it off and passed it back to him.

“Get the fuck outta here!” They all stood up and was ready to run.

"Youngbull!" Redz called out and he turned around to feel the flame from the .44

"BOOM BOOM BOOM!!!" He walked over to the dead body as the kid's homies looked at him leaking and not breathing. This wasn't what they expected.

"Y'all want my watch too right?"

"Nooo!" They both said in unison.

"Get the fuck outta here!" They turned and ran down the street happy they were spared.

"Text me babe!" Redz told Meeka who had tears in her eyes. She had never seen a dead body before, and there a body was on the sidewalk in front of her house. Redz hopped in the truck and J-jay sped off.

$ $ $ $ $ $ $ $ $ $ $ $ $ $ $ $ $

Moose and Tiffany were at his house in North East kissing heavy on the couch. Moose was playing with her pussy and she was soaking wet. He played with her clit as he sucked her neck. Tiffany was ready to explode, her insides were ready to erupt.

"Stop baby, stop hold up, I have to use the bathroom."

"What, can't it wait?" Moose said ready to fuck.

"No, I have to go I will be right back," Tiffany got up and went to the bathroom. She pulled the wire from under her breast and put it in her pocket. She was hot and Moose was ready to give her what she needed.

"I hope you ready for this Robin! I mean Tiffany, your Tiffany stay in character." She sad to herself. She opened the bathroom door and Moose was ass naked. He grabbed her and put his tongue deep in her throat. He started pulling her clothes off until she was in her birthday suit. He turned her around on the couch and pounded her with strokes from heaven. Every thrust made her body shake. She came after the first one reached the back of her vagina. He picked her up and took her to the bedroom. Moose laid her on her back and licked the sweat from her body. He then traveled to her inner thigh and pleased her with his tongue. She began to tremble as she twitched and came on his face. He wiped his mouth with his hand and licked her juices from his fingers.

“Damn you taste good,” Moose said and he entered her wetness. He pumped harder and faster as she splashed on his dick with her natural juices. This was the best sex she had ever had and she fell in love at that very moment. Moose came inside her as he fell on top of her sweaty body. They held one another and slept all night.

Tiffany was still sleep when Moose woke up. He went downstairs and cleaned up the mess they made. He started cooking breakfast for his sweet heart. He sat down for a second and picked her pants up off the floor. When he started to fold the pants something fell out of the pocket and hit the floor, he looked down at the small object and a thousand thoughts were running through his mind as he figured out what it was. *This is a fuckin wire he thought.* He checked the rest of her clothes and all she had was some gum and her i.d.He held the wire and fury and rage built up in his body, his blood was boiling he was so upset.

“Not my baby, please it can’t be. PLEASE GOD!!!! I finally found love.” He said out loud to himself. Moose walked to the bedroom and looked at his sleeping beauty.

“Tiff wake up, wake up Tiff,” she was out like a light. He shook her and she came to.

"What baby, what's wrong?" Tiffany said still half sleep.

"What's thisTiffany?" Moose held out the object in his hand.

Agent Jones jumped up in shock, she was at a lost for words.

"Please tell me you not a cop baby, tell me you not one of those pigs." He looked at her and she just started to cry. She really loved Moose and for the first time in her 6 year career, she had let her emotions get to her and she fell in love with the enemy.

"I'm sorry Moose, I'm an undercover agent. I was sent in to take the W.T.O organization down. I was suppose to get close and get information on Cash and Rome. Baby I fell in love with you, I really do love you." Agent Jones finally exposed herself like she wanted to do so many times before since their emotional attachment.

Moose began to let the tears fall. "You love me? You just killed me. I love you girl and this is what you do to me, you about to hit me with hundred years. I should have never let you get so close. I should kill you bitch, what do they know about us?"

"They know about Thompson Street, and you killing Tank. But I couldn't give them anything on Cash and Rome because I wasn't that close to them, so they don't really have shit on them solid. I'm the key to their case baby."

"They got me though. Have you been wired the whole time?"

"No, I took it off last night before we made love."

Moose started to cry, his heart was broken. He never felt this way about a woman in his life. This hurt like a knife through his chest. He had changed his life for a lie.

"I love you baby, come here give me a hug." Moose said and he grabbed her neck and put a deadly choke hold.

"Bitch you played me, you used me. You stomped on my heart, now you're going to die. Fuck you, and the rest of them pigs, you're going to hell while I do a hundred years. Diiiiiiiie!!"

Agent Jones was no match for the death lock he had around her throat with his huge arms. She began to stop fighting back as her life slowly slipped away. She heard Agent Galvin's voice before she passed out. "Never let your heart and emotions distract your mission. Never believe your cover always believe the objective." Moose kept choking her until she was stiff as a board.

"I love you," Moose said as he kissed her lifeless lips. Moose held her dead body in his arms as he dialed Cash's number.

"Ayo Cash bring the team to my house," Moose said as he rocked back and forth with Agent Jones in his arms.

"What's wrong?"

"Just do it," Moose yelled in the phone.

Cash hung up and got the team ready. They got there in twenty minutes and thoughout the trip they worried what was up. They walked in the house and saw Moose holding his girl's dead body.

"Ayo what happened?" Rome asked.

"She was an undercover for the Feds, they got me Cash. They wanted you and Rome but she only got close to me. I'm done cuz, I should have listened. I let her in too quick," Moose cried.

"Get this bitch to the bottom of the lake A.S.A.P," Cash yelled.

Jay-j and Redz took the body up and wrapped her in the rug on the floor.

"Get out of here before they kick this shit in. Go Moose get the fuck outta town," Rome said.

"I loved her Cash and she played me, now I know how them girls feel when we do them wrong. I feel like shit." Moose said still in a daze sitting on the floor looking up at his cousin. Cash shook his head.

"Ayo stop bitchin, we out, get ya shit and roll," Cash yelled.

Jay-j and Redz left with the body and Cash and Rome headed for the door.

"Call me so I can send you some money, we out," Cash said.

He and Rome left as Moose packed his bags. He knew it was only a matter of time before they came for him. He took his money from the safe in the floor and put it in a suitcase.

(Boom, Boom) Moose's door came crashing down. About twenty-five law inforcements, Swat and Federal agents came rushing in.....

"Freeze," one agent screamed.

“Put your hands up and come out of the bathroom now.” The agents yelled and Moose listened from in his room. They heard the shower water running and thought they had him trapped in the bathroom.

“Fuck these motherfuckers, I rather die than do life,” Moose thought as he put his bullet proof vest on and got his AK-47 from the closet. If it was a war he was going out blazing. They rushed the bathroom and no one was there. They slowly made their way to the bedrooms. They all stopped when they heard Moose yell from his room before they got there.

“Alright, I’m coming out don’t shoot, I don’t have any weapons,” Moose screamed. Swat was all in the hallway and agents were downstairs and outside the house. He was surrounded it was no way out for him.

“Here I come, I’m opening the door slowly,” Moose opened up the door and let out a wave of bullets from his machine gun. Bullets were flying everywhere as Swat fired at Moose and he fired back.

“Pull back, pull back,” the agents yelled. Moose stopped firing his gun, it was nothing coming from his room. The house was quiet as the smoke began to settle from all the gun fire. About four agents were down from the shots Moose let off, and more started toward the bedroom door. They carefully approached the room and one by one they were in the master bedroom 6 deep.Moose was nowhere. The closet door swung open from behind the agents

“Bahdddddddddddddd!!” The AK47 shot bullet after bullet as Moose took out about three agents and wounded the other two.

"You bitches can't fuck with a real gangsta, I did twenty motherfuckin years!!! I ain't going back!!! Fuck y'all, you gonna have to kill me before… Moose yells were cut short when a shot came through the window piercing his skull. The window in the bedroom cracked and one shot hit Moose in the back of the head. He hit the floor and blood poured from his forehead. More Agents came in the room with guns drawn. Moose was dead but he kept his promise to himself. He promised he would never see a cell again and he would hold court in the street. He would take as many as he could with him and meet God or the devil peacefully.

"Good shot," One officer said to the sniper who took Moose out. The sniper came back over the radio.

"I couldn't get a good shot. But it was murder she wrote when he stood in front of the window yelling."

The agents checked the house and didn't find agent Jones. They just found pictures of her and Moose, and two suitcases with 5 million dollars cash money in it. Special Agent Galvin came in the house as everything was all over. He couldn't believe how this turned out. His superiors were going to be all over him. His career could be over after this stunt, he had to get something on Cash before the week was out or he was done.

"Shit, this is a mess. How many are dead?" He asked as he walked upstairs and saw bodies and shell cases.

"It looks like eight sir, and six are wounded badly."

"God help me, these guys keep slipping away. He kills eight of my men and no sign of Agent Jones. I'm going to get fired, I'm dead when I get back to headquarters. Clear out and let the ambulance and forensics do their job. Get these men some medical attention A.S.A.P. This little shit Cash really thinks he is untouchable. I won't rest until I nail his ass. SHIIIIITTT!!" He screamed as he banged his fist against the door causing a crack in the wood. He put his dark shades on his face and walked out plotting his next attack. Cash would not slip away again and he would make sure of it. It was time to play dirty. He was going to get his man.

To Be Continued.....

Special Shout outs:

Special shout out to West Philly and the city of Philadelphia in whole as the city that made me. Real niggas come first. P.I.P E.B and my best friend Ollie! Shout out my right hand J-Jay, my bro and my partner Musa Small Aka Moose. My Brother from another P.T you already know! Free Smoke Hold your head my nigga, the streets miss you. G.H.I and the whole B.A.U. family, they my boys! Deadbroke Chevy car club. The Dirty Block 49th Thompson all my niggas already know / F-block(Felton Street)

Special Shout out my cousin Rell, miss you cuz. He couldn't be here to see this come out. R.I.P (Gone But Never Forgotten) I love you and I'm mad we just talked before they took you away. It just doesn't seem real. Tell Ernest I said whassup and I'm a hold it down until we meet again.

Made in the USA
Charleston, SC
26 March 2013